D0360828

Pig removed the foil from the can. After giving the sticky ointment inside another stir, he carefully rubbed a little of it onto his left hand.

Yes!

Muttering the rest of the spell, he watched his fingers shorten, his palm thicken, his nails become claws.

It works—it really works!

My Brother, the WEREWOLF

by Nancy Garden

BULLSEYE BOOKS

Random House   New York

A BULLSEYE BOOK PUBLISHED BY RANDOM HOUSE, INC.

Copyright © 1995 by Nancy Garden.
Cover art copyright © 1995 by Broeck Steadman.
All rights reserved under International and Pan-American Copyright
Conventions. Published in the United States by Random House, Inc.,
New York, and simultaneously in Canada by Random House of
Canada Limited, Toronto.

Library of Congress Cataloging-in-Publication Data:
Garden, Nancy.   My brother, the werewolf / by Nancy Garden.   p.   cm.
Summary: Twelve-year-old Frankie discovers horrifying evidence that her
younger brother, Pig, is experimenting with shapeshifting into a
dangerous animal.
ISBN 0-679-85414-2 (pbk.) — ISBN 0-679-95414-7 (lib. bdg.)
[1. Werewolves—Fiction. 2. Horror stories.] I. Title. PZ7.G165Mv
1995 [Fic]—dc20 93-46795

RL: 5.0

Manufactured in the United States of America
10 9 8 7 6 5 4 3 2 1

PROLOGUE

Quietly now...

Pig Davis crept out of bed in his shadow-filled room and into the upstairs hall of his house in Cambridge, Massachusetts. He listened outside his parents' bedroom door. Dad was snoring. Mom was breathing deeply and regularly. Then he looked into his older sister, Frankie's, room. Frankie was curled up into a tight ball, with the family cat, Mouser, a small calico, purring by her side.

Yes, it's safe.

Pig—Paul, actually, but his family called him Pig because of his huge appetite—went back to his room. Flipping on the computer, he carefully put some dog hair he'd collected from a neighbor's pet into his pajama pocket. Then he punched the keyboard and pored over the list of plants that appeared on the

1

screen. Finally he took a bowl of foul-smelling ointment down from his bureau.

"Cinquefoil," he whispered, taking a dry greenish sprig from his top drawer and crumbling it into the goo in the bowl.

That's why it didn't work last time. I forgot to add the cinquefoil.

He stirred the mixture, grinning as he remembered the dubious look on the face of the man in the dingy little back-street herb shop where he'd bought most of his ingredients. "If I didn't know better, sonny," the man had said, "I'd think you were making some kind of witch's brew. What's this for, anyway?"

"Chemistry class," Pig had said quickly, just as he'd planned to say if anyone asked him. "I'm studying chemistry."

"A bit young, aren't you?" the man said, putting the little plastic envelopes of plant material into a bag.

"It's a special class," Pig lied. "For gifted kids. You know."

The herb man didn't argue. But what if he had? What if Pig had had to tell the truth?

The man wouldn't have believed him.

No one would.

Pig put some of the goo in an empty cat food can, covered the can with a piece of aluminum foil, and switched off the computer.

He quietly eased his window open. Then he climbed carefully down the wisteria vine outside it, dropped almost noiselessly into the backyard, and whispered:

"Far, far away under the bright moon,
 In the wide space under the stars,
 Birch and oak and stream watch
As the circle forms and the ancient
   words are spoken,
And as we apply the essence, the sacred
   essence,
 Giver of freedom, of life, of power and
   strength…"

Pig removed the foil from the can. After giving the sticky mess another stir, he carefully rubbed a little of it onto his left hand.

Yes!

But it wasn't over yet. Muttering the rest of the spell, he watched his fingers shorten, his palm thicken, his nails become claws. It was amazing how quickly he had transformed himself.

It works—it really works! he thought excitedly.

CHAPTER 1

Brawk! Brawk! *Brawk!*

The horrible cry woke Frankie—short for Frances—Davis out of a sound sleep and made her sit straight up in bed. Blinking, her cat, Mouser, also sat up.

Bewildered, Frankie looked around the strange room. Where was her tall white dresser? Why wasn't it between the two windows, where it belonged? Where, for that matter, was the second window? And why was bright moonlight streaming into the room instead of the usual soft glow from the streetlight outside?

Slowly Frankie remembered. She wasn't at home in Cambridge with traffic whizzing by and city sounds all around. Instead, she and her eleven-year-old brother, Pig, were at Dunmead, their uncle's chicken farm in New

4

Hampshire. Their parents were vacationing on their boat somewhere off the coast of Maine, the way they did every summer.

Brawk!

There it was again. This time, Mouser leaped off the bed and scrambled underneath it, obviously scared stiff.

Frankie got up and padded across the wide pine floorboards to the window. The farmyard was completely bathed in moonlight. She couldn't see anything unusual in the yard. There was the big oak tree by the fence, and Aunt Trina's flower garden near the driveway, with her vegetable garden beyond. In the distance Frankie could see the long, low henhouse, and the wire fence around the chicken yard. The barn's squat form rose behind them, same as always.

Frankie shrugged and went back to bed, snuggling under the covers. She loved visiting the farm.

The best part was being with her cousin Ben, who was twelve like her. Ben was one of Frankie's best friends. The only bad part was being without TV, which Uncle Joe and Aunt Trina wouldn't allow in the house. "Television rots the mind," Uncle Joe was always saying.

That was okay for Uncle Joe, who liked to

spend his evenings strumming his guitar and singing the folk songs he wrote in his spare time. But ever since Frankie had decided last fall, at the beginning of seventh grade, that she wanted to be a news photographer, she'd spent *her* spare time studying photos in newspapers and watching documentaries on TV. And she'd asked for and gotten a good still camera for her birthday, which she couldn't wait to try out at the farm.

Brawk!

There was that noise again—the hens were squawking louder now. Frankie heard Uncle Joe stomping down the stairs, muttering. She got out of bed, threw on her bathrobe, grabbed her camera and its flash attachment, and followed him.

Brawkbrawkbrawk!

"Coming, coming," Uncle Joe was mumbling sleepily as Frankie caught up with him. He pulled a blue flannel shirt on over his pajamas and grabbed a flashlight off the kitchen counter. "Hello, Frankie," he said, glancing at her. "Come to see what the ruckus is about? Poor old hens! They get upset at the slightest thing." He quickly opened the back door.

They ran past the gardens and soon reached the chicken yard fence. The nearly full moon cast pale white light over the farm buildings, giving the entire scene an eerie glow.

From inside the henhouse came a frantic squawking and fluttering.

"Look!" shouted Frankie, catching a dim glimpse of something furry disappearing around the far corner of the henhouse, inside the fence. It looked like a dog's tail.

"Hey! Get out of there!" Uncle Joe shouted angrily, breaking into a run as Frankie aimed her camera at the dog's back end—but it was too late. By the time Uncle Joe and Frankie got to the far corner, the animal had vanished.

Ben, with Thrip, the farm dog, beside him, suddenly appeared from behind the henhouse. His black hair was tousled and his freckles stood out sharply in the beam of Uncle Joe's flashlight. "I think I hit it!" he shouted breathlessly.

"What was it?" asked Uncle Joe.

"A big dog, I think," said Ben. "Gray. Kind of slinky. I pitched a rock at it, and I think I hit one of its front legs. And then Thrip chased it off." He reached down and fondled the dog's ears. "Well, he ran after it for a minute, anyway, when it got outside the fence. There's a hole— it must've dug in. Thrip didn't seem too eager to go after it. Maybe it was a dog he knows."

Thrip was a friendly black Labrador retriever. He was a good watchdog, and very obedient—except that he liked to chase chickens, so he was often out of favor with Uncle Joe.

"We'd better check the fence, then," Uncle Joe said. He looked wide awake now—and very worried—as he led them along the edge of the chicken yard, closely examining the wire fence as he walked. Frankie knew that a marauding animal could scare hens so much they wouldn't lay eggs. So even if the dog hadn't actually attacked them, it could have done a lot of damage. Uncle Joe and Aunt Trina depended on eggs for most of their income.

Ahead of Frankie, Uncle Joe and Ben suddenly bent down. There was a hole in the ground, Frankie saw when she caught up to them—quite a large one, under the fence and on both sides of it. Around the hole, the wire was puckered and pushed out.

"I was right," Ben said. "The dog must've dug in and then crawled out the same way."

Uncle Joe pulled the fence back into place and scraped loose dirt into the hole with his foot. "We'll fix this properly in the morning," he said. "Let's have a look inside the henhouse. Sit, Thrip. Stay."

Thrip sat obediently outside the henhouse door, and Frankie followed her uncle and cousin.

Uncle Joe switched on the light. The hens were still clucking nervously and flapping around on their roosts. Feathers were strewn on the floor, especially in a far corner. Frankie went over to investigate as Uncle Joe and Ben walked slowly down the center aisle, one on each side, checking the hens and talking softly to them.

"I guess Thrip and I got here in time," Ben said. "I don't think that animal got in at all."

"Yes, it did," Frankie said, noticing a pile of bloody feathers under one of the roosts. "Look." She took a quick picture.

Uncle Joe and Ben hurried to her side.

"Whoa!" said Ben softly. "It sure did get in."

Angrily, Uncle Joe scooped up the pile of feathers, then reached for the wounded hen that was huddled on the roost above. She wasn't moving. "Shhh, biddy, biddy, biddy," he crooned. "Shh." Stroking the hen, he examined her. Frankie winced when she saw the hen's bloody back and side.

Uncle Joe tucked the wounded bird under his arm. "Well, ladies," he said, addressing the other hens, "you had ample reason to squawk. Squawk again if anything disturbs you, okay?" He patted the hen he held. "She'll be okay, I think," he said. "Especially after we clean her up. But we'd better do that soon, before the

9

wound gets infected." He headed for the door, and Frankie followed with Ben.

"I wonder why the dog didn't just kill her," Ben said as they left the henhouse.

"Maybe you interrupted him," said Uncle Joe. "Thank goodness. I'm going to go in and see to the hen," he went on. "And I'll try to convince Trina that it's breakfast time. No point in going back to bed now that it's almost dawn. Ben," he added, "tie Thrip up outside before you come in, okay? He'll warn us if that other dog comes back—not that he's likely to in daylight."

"Other dog...or what*ever*," Ben said to Frankie when his father had left. "I'm not sure it *was* a dog."

"How come?" asked Frankie. "It looked like a dog to me—what I saw of it, anyway."

"I heard it before I saw it," Ben told her. "Well, I heard Thrip first. He started sort of moaning and snuffling. Then he scratched at my bedroom door, so I got up and opened it, and he went *flying* down the stairs. I followed him, and then I heard the squawks. Thrip ran to the back door and when I let him out he took off like a bullet for the henhouse. He would've gone right through the screen door if I hadn't gotten there as fast as I did."

"What about Pig?" Frankie asked. Her

brother was sharing Ben's room. "Didn't he wake up, too?"

"I guess he slept through it," Ben answered with a shrug. "At least he didn't say anything or move." He grinned. "He was up late working on his computer, so he must've been pretty tired."

Frankie nodded. That would be just like Pig, who had insisted on taking the family's computer to the farm. For some time before they'd left Cambridge, he'd spent hours in front of the small gray screen, working on what he called his Special Project.

"Anyway, Thrip and I ran out," Ben went on, "and I saw something by the henhouse door. I forgot to bring a flashlight, so I couldn't really tell what it was, even in the moonlight, but it looked like some kind of big dog. Thrip ran toward it—but here's the weird part. He ran almost to the fence, but all of a sudden he stopped and looked back at me, and whined. By then the—the whatever—was running around the back of the henhouse. I said, 'Go get it, boy!' and opened the gate. Well, you know how Thrip is. He always does what he's told, and he did go after it, but not the way a dog does when it really wants to chase something. It was like—like he was scared, almost."

"But Thrip's never scared!" Frankie exclaimed, surprised. "Of anything."

"No, he's not. At least not that I can remember. The animal did look like a big dog—a huge one. Kind of grayish, with long hair, a long tail, and a long nose, not a blunt one like Thrip's. More like a German shepherd nose."

While Ben described the animal, Frankie felt something furry brush against her leg. She jumped, then saw it was Thrip. Still, she felt spooked.

"Thrip!" Ben cried. "Hey—what's the matter, boy?"

Frankie turned, and saw Thrip trembling. The dog pressed tightly against Ben, his eyes wild, as if he were terrified.

CHAPTER 2

Quick—oh, ouch—leg hurts—but quick, run now, run swiftly in the moonlight, race like the wind away from the hens, from the stinging thing—run—run…

There now. Safe.

Pig paused, panting, and spat bloody chicken feathers out of his mouth. They stuck between his teeth; he had to poke them out with his tongue.

But it was fun.

His eyes gleamed red in the moonlight as he remembered how he'd chased them—first one, then another—darting, snatching—grabbing one—till the person came, and the dog, and the stinging thing.

What was it?

Pig lifted his arm—now a front leg, covered with thick coarse gray hair. He thought he wanted to *see* the stinging wound he'd felt on it back in the chicken yard, but *sniffing* it came more naturally, for some reason.

Blood again.

He licked it.

Salty. Nice!

A little stiffly, Pig loped deeper into the woods near Dunmead Farm, his long wolf shape making a dark shadow on the moonlit path.

By the time Frankie and Ben had calmed Thrip down enough to tie him up outside and go back to the house, the sun was almost all the way up and Aunt Trina and Uncle Joe were in the kitchen. The injured hen, her wounds cleaned, was resting in a cardboard box near the stove.

"Breakfast's almost ready," Uncle Joe said.

"Great!" said Ben. "I'm starved." He pulled out a chair and sat down at the big oak table that dominated the room.

"I'll get Pig," said Frankie.

"Paul's not with you?" Aunt Trina turned away from the stove, where Frankie saw a huge pan of scrambled eggs and a platter of perfectly cooked bacon. "I went to call him, and he wasn't in his room. But the computer was on, so I thought he must be up. I figured he'd gone out to find you."

"Maybe he's just in the bathroom," Frankie said. "I'll go see." She ran upstairs.

But Pig wasn't in the bathroom. Well, Frankie thought, maybe he'd been there when Aunt Trina looked for him, and then had gone back to finish whatever he was doing on the computer. Maybe he'd even gone back to bed.

Frankie was sure for a moment she was right, for as soon as she went into the room Pig shared with Ben, she saw a Pig-sized lump in his bed. "There you are, lazy!" she called, going over to it. "Come on, get up. It's time for breakfast." She reached out to shake him— and felt only a pillow.

"What in…?" Frankie stripped back the covers and saw that Pig had put his pillow and a rolled-up blanket lengthwise under them, so it looked as if he were in the bed. *Why is he being so sneaky?*

Frowning, she went over to the computer, which was perched at one end of Ben's desk. It was on, as Aunt Trina had said. There was a list on the screen:

Aconite
Hemlock

Oak
Belladonna
Nightshade
Poplar
Cinquefoil
Sweet flag
Henbane
Parsley

Since when is Pig interested in plants? At least, Frankie thought those were all plants. She wasn't too sure about a few—aconite, for example, and sweet flag—but she had no doubt about ones like oak and parsley. She scanned the books on the desk for something of Pig's that might tell her what the list was about, but all the books were about stars and planets. Ben wanted to be an astronomer, and had spent last summer trying unsuccessfully to build a telescope. This summer he was making a huge star chart. Markers, rolled-up paper, rulers, and protractors were scattered among the books.

On the chair by Pig's bed were the jeans he'd worn the day before, and the green T-shirt he'd put on after dinner; he'd spilled spaghetti sauce on the shirt he'd been wearing and Aunt Trina had made him change. His slippers were beside the bed, but his high-tops were missing, and his pajamas were nowhere in sight. His bathrobe—another concession to Aunt Trina—was hanging on the bedpost.

Why, Frankie wondered, would he put on his high-tops if he was still wearing his pajamas?

To go outside?

But if he'd gone outside, she reasoned, it would probably have been because of the ruckus in the henhouse.

Then why hadn't she seen him?

On the table beside the bed, next to the lamp and a computer magazine, was a medium-sized bowl. "Yuck, old cereal," Frankie said out loud. But when she looked more closely, expecting to see soggy flakes and scummy milk, she saw disgusting greenish lumpy goo. She held it up to her nose. It smelled like old rotting leaves and grass.

Still trying to figure things out, Frankie went to her own room to see if by any chance Pig was there looking for her. He wasn't, but Mouser was still cowering under the bed. "Come on, kitty," Frankie said, kneeling and waggling her fingers at the cat. "Come on. It's safe."

Mouser purred and blinked, but she didn't move.

Frankie found Mouser's favorite catnip

mouse wrapped up in her tangled sheet. Lying across the bed on her stomach, she dangled it by the tail over the edge. "Mouser, come on. Kitty, kitty, kitty!"

Slowly Mouser edged closer…closer…

"Frankie, what *are* you doing?"

Mouser suddenly yowled and scurried under the bed again, farther back than before.

Frankie stood up so quickly that she felt a little dizzy.

Pig, in his pajamas, carrying his high-tops, and wearing a fur cap Frankie had never seen before, was standing at the door to her room. His face was smudged and scratched, and he was cradling one arm in the other, as if it hurt.

Frankie scrambled off the bed and onto her feet. "What happened to you?" she asked. "Where were you? Everyone's looking for you. Some animal scared the hens, and—"

"Yeah," Pig said vaguely. "I know. I went out, too." He leaned down and peered under the bed. "Hi, Mouser," he said.

Mouser, with a loud, terrified hiss, shot out the side opposite Pig, skirted him widely, and disappeared down the hall.

What's with her? Frankie wondered. Both Mouser and Pig were acting very strange, and she had no idea why.

CHAPTER 3

"I tripped and fell on a rock," Pig explained a few minutes later in the kitchen. He had his bathrobe on now, and was sitting at the table while Aunt Trina examined his arm, on which there was a rapidly darkening bruise. Frankie could see that the cuffs of his pajama pants were dirty, and that his ankles were scratched and covered with mud. He winced when Aunt Trina touched his arm.

"Yes, but what were you doing outside in the first place?" Aunt Trina opened the freezer and got out some ice, which she wrapped in a dish towel and handed to Uncle Joe. "Would you crush this, please?" she asked him.

Uncle Joe disappeared into the mud room off the kitchen, and Frankie could hear him smashing the ice.

"Huh?" Pig blinked sleepily, still cradling his arm.

"What were you doing outside in the first place?" Aunt Trina asked again.

"I—er—I went out with Thrip," Pig said, looking at the floor. "He—um—he woke me up and asked to go out. You know. Barked. Scratched."

Frankie stared at her brother. He'd never been a good liar—he hardly ever lied at all—and it was obvious he was lying now. But why?

Aunt Trina exchanged a glance with Uncle Joe as he came back and handed her the ice-filled towel. But she didn't say anything; she just held the towel against Pig's arm.

"But *I* let Thrip out!" Ben exclaimed indignantly. "You were asleep."

"Well, I—I must have let him out a second time," Pig insisted. "After you did."

"Oh, come on," said Uncle Joe. "Then who let him in, between the two times? Look, Paul," he said kindly, "it's okay if you went out, for a walk or whatever. I do that myself sometimes when I can't sleep—although now, with a strange animal around and going after the hens, it's probably not a good idea for any of us to take midnight walks for a while. Anyway, no one's blaming you for anything. It's only that we want to know what happened. That's all. I mean, you did get hurt...."

"I just tripped," Pig said again. "It's okay, really." He smiled at Aunt Trina. "Thanks for the ice. It feels better now. I don't think it's broken or anything."

"No," said Uncle Joe. "I don't either, and I'm glad of that." He bent down so his head was level with Pig's. "You must've been in the barn," he said, "since you found my old cap." He touched the furry cap, which was still on Pig's head.

"That was earlier," Pig said, looking uncomfortable. "Yesterday afternoon. I meant to ask—sorry, Uncle Joe. I hope it's okay that I took it."

"You should have asked first," Uncle Joe said. "But it's okay. Just don't lose it. I made it myself, out of a wolf's pelt when I was a boy in Alaska." He straightened up and went to the window, looking out over the now-sunny farmyard. "And I'll make a coyote one soon, if that animal comes back and bothers my hens again."

"So...you think it was a coyote, then?" asked Ben. He helped himself to a couple of biscuits and slathered them with butter. "But I didn't think there were any of those around here."

"I dunno," said Uncle Joe. "From your description, I'd say there's a good chance of it—a good old Eastern coyote, down from Canada, maybe, or over from Maine. Of course it could be someone's dog gone bad. That does happen, but it'd have to be a stray. I'm pretty sure I know all the dogs around here. And the only one that I'd suspect might go after chickens is kept tied up."

"Lobo, right?" asked Ben.

"Right." Uncle Joe took a biscuit from the platter and poured honey on it.

"Who's Lobo?" asked Frankie. She glanced at Pig, who was scarfing down his food. He was on his fourth or fifth strip of bacon. At least *that* was normal for him.

But he seemed edgy somehow, as if he didn't want to be there.

"Oh," said Uncle Joe, "Lobo belongs to a neighbor, Ken Taylor, who's kind of standoffish. Ken doesn't get along with very many people, and Lobo takes after him. The dog's part wolf, actually, and looks like what Ben described. But he's been tied up ever since he went after someone's sheep, long ago."

"Yeah, but what if he got loose?" Ben asked.

Uncle Joe laughed. "He's not a young dog any more. And he was pretty lazy last time I saw him. I doubt it was old Lobo." He took another biscuit. "If the animal comes back," he said to Frankie, "maybe you could take a picture of it with that fancy camera of yours."

"Sure," said Frankie eagerly. "It's got a pretty good flash. I would've gotten one before if the animal hadn't run away so fast."

Pig glanced at her, an uneasy look in his eyes.

After breakfast, Uncle Joe announced that he wanted to clean up the henhouse and then try to animal-proof it. "Any offers of help," he said, pushing his chair back, "will be gratefully accepted."

"I'll help," said Frankie.

"Me, too," said Ben. "Pig?"

"I—er—no," Pig said evasively. "I mean... I've got something else I have to do."

"What do you have to do?" Frankie asked.

Pig glared at her. "Something private," he said, getting up from the table. "Mind your own business." He went upstairs, his feet pounding on each step.

"That doesn't seem like Paul!" said Aunt Trina, looking worried. "You two always get along so well."

"He's probably just sleepy," Uncle Joe said cheerfully. "Probably couldn't get back to sleep after being out with Thrip and hurting

23

his arm on the rock and all." He pushed his chair back and stood. "Coming, work crew?"

Frankie and Ben got up, but Aunt Trina held Frankie back. "Frankie," she asked when Ben and Uncle Joe had left, "has your brother ever walked in his sleep?"

"Not that I know of," Frankie answered, startled.

"Are you sure? I mean, it's obvious that he was outside last night, only I don't quite believe his explanation of how he got there. I'm pretty sure it was Ben who let Thrip out."

"Yeah," said Frankie thoughtfully. "So am I. I don't think he ever *used* to sleepwalk," she continued, her hand on the door.

Still, her brother was being unusually grumpy that morning. Had he sleepwalked— or was something else bothering him?

But we've both always loved staying at the farm, Frankie thought. *How could anything possibly bother Pig here?*

CHAPTER 4

"Come on, Mouser," Frankie said, on her way to the hen-house. She squatted down and waggled her fingers at her cat, who was huddled under the porch. "Come on, kitty. It's safe. Really it is. Come on!"

Mouser rolled coyly onto her back, just out of reach.

"Oh, come on," said Frankie. "I'll rub your tummy if you come out."

Mouser purred loudly and rolled back onto her front. Then she crept out slowly, one dainty white paw at a time. Finally she let Frankie pick her up and cuddle her.

But as soon as Pig approached, carrying an old-looking book, Mouser stopped purring and leaped out of Frankie's arms, hissing.

Pig stared after her with an odd look on his face.

"Now look what you've done," Frankie said angrily. "You scared her, popping up like that."

"I did not pop up," Pig said. "She's just being weird, is all."

"Seems to me you're the one who's being weird," Frankie retorted. "Aunt Trina just asked me if you sleepwalk. You don't, do you?"

Pig seemed startled. "No," he said. "Of course not."

Frankie looked closely at his eyes; they looked odd—harsh, somehow. They made her feel strange inside; she didn't like looking at them, yet she felt strangely drawn to them.

She looked away. "That was a pretty fake story you told everyone at breakfast," she said, trying to pull herself together. "How come?"

For a moment Pig stared at her; she watched his mouth instead of his eyes, but even so she could feel his gaze burning into her. Then, abruptly, he turned aside. "I thought I told you to mind your own business," he said curtly, and bolted away.

Busybody Frankie—nosy sister—who needs her, anyway? Sleepwalking! Right!

Better be careful, though.

Pig made his way to the beech tree that grew on the side of the farmhouse away from the chicken yard. There he sat down, leaning

26

his back against the beech's massive trunk.

So it's really working, he thought. *The oint-ment and the cap and everything. Wow!*

He felt excited, even exhilarated.

But in some small corner of his mind, he also felt a little scared. Maybe more scared, even, than when he'd started.

Don't be scared. That's silly. This is special; no one else can do it. No one else has dared for years and years—centuries, maybe. Hey, Paul Davis, he thought, *you can do some-thing nobody else can do! Frankie can take pictures, and Ben knows all about stars, and Mom and Dad can sail. But I, Paul Davis— Pig—can...turn myself into something else.*

His stomach growled hungrily.

Bacon's not enough. Not nearly enough. When's lunch?

He looked down at his wrist, but his watch was gone. Annoyed, he remembered stuffing it into the pocket of his pajama top when he'd...changed. And putting it on his bureau when he got back in the morning.

Drat! Well, I'll get it later.

Pig opened the book he'd gotten out of the library right before they'd left Cambridge. The thick pages were yellow with age, and the long, complicated sentences used big words like lycanthropy and *lobis-homem*. Pig struggled to understand them, skipping over accounts of medieval witchcraft trials that should have been interesting but weren't. After a while, he closed the book and walked back to the house to put it away and get his watch.

The watch was on his bureau, just as he'd thought, but a little gray hair had gotten caught in the band. It came back to him then that he'd almost forgotten about his watch the night before. He'd remembered it at the last minute, and then he'd torn it off with his teeth.

Just in time, too!

It had been tight, constricting; no wonder some hair had caught in it.

Got to be careful of that, he thought, slipping the band back around his wrist. *Got to take it off sooner.*

The watch showed him it was only ten-thirty, a long way from lunch. *Still*, he thought, making his way downstairs, *maybe Aunt Trina's got something worth eating.*

But Aunt Trina wasn't in the kitchen when he got there. From the sound of it, she was cleaning the living room.

Well, she won't mind.

Pig opened the refrigerator and looked at everything inside: leftover noodles, pickles, jam, eggs, butter, milk, soda, half an apple pie, cheese…bacon! He quickly peeled off a strip.

It was almost good, even raw.

But not quite.

The small piece of leftover ham that he found behind a bowl of quivering red Jell-O was good, though.

But there wasn't enough to satisfy the gnawing in his stomach. Not nearly enough.

He went outside again, onto the porch.

He could hear Uncle Joe, Frankie, and Ben talking and laughing as they worked, so he wandered toward the chicken yard, then frowned.

Uncle Joe was near the hole under the fence, with a shovel and a pair of pliers.

No! Pig thought with sudden alarm, anger swelling inside him. *No, stop!*

Shouldn't—don't fix fence. No—no!

His lips pulled back from his teeth and his hands clenched into tight fists. A low growling sound rose in his throat.

Drawn toward his uncle by a power he couldn't control, Pig moved slowly forward, stiffly, his lips still curled back and his eyes blazing—

"Paul!" Aunt Trina called from the porch. "There you are. Come help me move the piano, would you, so I can clean behind it?"

Pig shook himself. *Whoa. That was close.*

All that morning, while she gathered eggs and helped clean and animal-proof the henhouse, Frankie racked her brain to sort out what was going on with her brother.

First of all, there was no doubt that, sleepwalking or no sleepwalking, Pig was acting strange.

Second, how had he hurt his arm?

If he *had* been sleepwalking, could he have gone so far away that he really wouldn't have been able to hear the commotion in the henhouse?

If he hadn't been sleepwalking, what had he been doing outside in the middle of the night—again, so far away that he hadn't heard the hens?

Or *had* he heard them?

None of it made any sense.

CHAPTER 5

"Break time!" Uncle Joe called. While Frankie and Ben worked inside the henhouse, he'd dug up the bottom of the wire fence, which was buried a few inches underground. After finishing up in the henhouse, Frankie and Ben had helped him bury it deeper, especially near the filled-in hole, where they'd found a few doglike paw prints.

Now Uncle Joe straightened up and went into the henhouse. Frankie and Ben followed. "It looks great in here," Uncle Joe said, glancing around. "You've done a terrific job, kids. Any whole eggs?"

Frankie held up the gathering basket. "About a dozen. There were lots of smashed ones, and lots of empty nests."

Uncle Joe nodded. "Too scared to lay," he said with a sigh. "Well, I'll just have to explain to my buyer. But things should be okay tomorrow if we have a quiet night. I think we've fixed it so nothing can get into the chicken yard. I guess I didn't bury the bottom of the fence deep enough when I first put it up." He put one arm over Frankie's shoulder and the other over Ben's. "You kids deserve a break," he said as they walked back toward the house. "Why don't you fix a picnic lunch and go down to the pond to cool off?"

"We'll go down to the pond later, Dad," Ben said. "But I want to check out those paw prints first."

Uncle Joe shrugged. "Suit yourself. If it *is* a coyote, I don't think you'll see him in broad daylight. But be careful. If you do see him, just notice where he is and come back. Don't disturb him. Coming, Frankie?"

"I think I'll go with Ben," she said.

"Suit yourself," Uncle Joe said again. "But you be careful, too." He gave them a wave as he strode off toward the house.

The paw prints were in the soft dirt on the other side of the fence, a little beyond the filled-in hole.

"I think we can follow them," Ben said after examining them for a few minutes, "if we look carefully. It's a good thing it rained a couple of days ago," he added. "If the ground had been really dry, there wouldn't have been any prints. Come on!" He and Frankie hurried out through the chicken yard gate and doubled back along the fence to where the paw prints were. "The prints are pretty clear, at least some of them."

"Here's another," said Frankie, moving slowly toward the woods, studying the ground. "And another."

They crept forward, one of them staying with each new print they found while the other went ahead searching for the next. There weren't many paw prints, and they didn't go in anything resembling a straight line, but there were enough to follow. The trail wound through the woods to a clearing— a muddy, grassless spot surrounded by birch and ash trees, with a small brook to one side.

"This is the brook that runs into our swimming pond," said Ben.

Frankie examined the ground more closely. Suddenly she saw what looked like athletic shoe prints coming in from near the brook and going into the clearing, where they seemed to go around in a circle, sometimes with paw prints alongside them.

"Look, Ben," she said, shocked. "It's like there was a *person* with the animal! At least for a while, anyway."

"You're right." Ben peered down at the prints, then glanced up at Frankie. "Pig?" he asked softly, looking puzzled.

"I—I don't know." Frankie felt as puzzled as Ben looked. "I mean, we know he was out last night and all, but why? If the paw prints belong to the animal that scared the chickens, why would Pig be with it? And if he'd chased it or followed it or something, why wouldn't he have told us about it?"

"Beats me," Ben said, frowning. "But there *are* shoe prints, and the pattern on them looks kind of like the pattern on the bottoms of the shoes Pig wears, and"—he put his foot in one—"they're about the right size, too."

"But," said Frankie, "it doesn't look as if there are any shoe prints leading *out* of the clearing. There'd have to be, wouldn't there, for Pig, or whoever it was, to get *back*."

"Yeah," said Ben, "but they do seem to come from near the brook, which does go to our pond."

Frankie ran over to the brook. "They just sort of fade away here!" she shouted to Ben. "There's lot of leaves, though. I guess that's why there aren't any prints."

"Yeah, but come here," Ben called. "The animal ones leave the clearing. Looks like they're even on a path."

Frankie joined him, and they both headed down the path.

"Oh, no!" Ben exclaimed suddenly, after they'd gone about fifty yards. He grabbed Frankie's arm. "I know where we are!"

"Where?" Frankie asked, blinking. The trees had thinned out again, and she and Ben stood at the edge of someone's very sunny backyard.

"The Taylors' place," said Ben in a low voice, almost a whisper. "They're—like Dad said, they don't get along with people too well. And they're the ones with that wolf-dog, Lobo. They've also got a kid, Hank, who's— Oh, no!"

Coming toward them was a large, long-haired gray dog with a pointy nose. Right behind him was a boy about their age, with a scowl on his face and a stout stick in his hand. Frankie was relieved when she noticed he was wearing high-top athletic shoes like Pig's. It was all starting to come together—the footprints, the paw prints, the gray tail she'd seen....

"You're trespassing, Ben Brooke!" the boy called. His tone was nasty. "Give me one good reason why I shouldn't set my dog on you."

Ben pulled himself up to his full height, which was quite a bit shorter than the other boy's. "We were just following some paw prints, Hank," he said loudly, showing no fear. "We didn't know they'd lead to your place. But they seem to go from our chicken yard to here. Where was Lobo last night?"

"In his doghouse, where he always is," said Hank. "Tied up. Sit, Lobo."

The wolf-dog sat, but he watched them suspiciously, his tongue lolling out of his mouth and his expression steely hard.

"You're sure he was tied up?" Frankie managed to ask.

"Who are you?" Hank's eyes narrowed unpleasantly as he stared at her.

"Frankie Davis," she said. "Ben's cousin. Last night Ben and I saw a big gray dog in my uncle's chicken yard, scaring the hens half to death. The dog hurt one of them, too."

"You'd better be sure Lobo was tied," warned Ben. "You know what happens around here to dogs that go after chickens. Especially if everyone knows they're part wolf to begin with."

"Lobo," said Hank, stepping closer, "wouldn't be bothered with anyone's chickens, let alone your dad's scrawny ones. But he *would* be bothered with you if you came around here again. Now get off my property!" He raised his stick menacingly.

"You just keep him tied," said Ben calmly. "Come on, Frankie."

"Wow!" said Frankie as she and Ben hurried back down the path. "I wouldn't want to meet either of *them* on a dark night!"

"I don't even like meeting them in the day-time," said Ben. "Hank's a jerk." He turned toward her. "The thing is that those pawprints led right to the Taylors'. It's got to have been Lobo we saw last night."

"And," said Frankie, "since there were those shoe prints, made by sneakers just like the ones Hank was wearing..."

Ben nodded. "It's almost as if Hank took Lobo to the clearing and let him go."

"Maybe," said Frankie. "But we didn't see any shoe prints going to or coming from the Taylors'. We only saw them in the clearing and coming from the side near the brook."

"True," Ben acknowledged. "But the prints along the path were kind of messy. There could have been shoe prints there along with the dog prints."

"I hope so," Frankie said. "Because if there aren't, then everything points to Pig again."

Ben shook his head. "Not really," he said. "Pig doesn't have any reason for doing some-thing like this. And where would he get a strange dog? It's just a coincidence that he was out last night, too."

"Yeah, maybe," said Frankie dubiously, "but Hank doesn't have any motive either—does he?"

"Sure he does," Ben told her. "His dad doesn't get along with anyone, like my dad said. And Hank and I had a fight at the end of school this year. He wanted to copy off me during a test and I wouldn't let him. That was only a few weeks ago. *And*," he added triumphantly, "Hank's got a big gray dog, part wolf. It fits perfectly."

"I hope so," Frankie said. "I just wish we could *prove* it, for sure."

"Maybe we can," Ben said thoughtfully. "Maybe we could get Lobo's paw print and match it to the prints in the chicken yard."

Frankie considered that for a minute as they walked along. "It's a neat idea," she said slowly. "But how are we going to do it?"

"I don't know. Maybe we could steal him."

"He doesn't look very stealable."

"No, he doesn't," Ben admitted.

"Besides," Frankie said as they came out of the woods near the farmhouse, "it's not like he's the kind of dog you can just go up to and— Hey, wait a sec! They keep him outside at night, right?"

"Right."

"Well, okay. He's got to sleep sometime, right?"

"Right," Ben said again.

"So maybe we could wait till he's asleep and then sneak up to him and stick his foot in wet cement or something to make a print of it. We did it in art class once, with hands. Making a cast, it's called."

"Good idea," Ben said. "But a lot easier said than done. Remember, Lobo's not exactly friendly."

"Yeah," said Frankie, getting excited about the idea now, "but maybe we could lure him with food. Look, there's got to be a way! If we can prove it's Lobo that went after your dad's hens, then maybe your dad could get Hank's parents to keep Lobo inside, or at least tied up better."

"Okay, you're on. Let's try it, anyway, tonight." Ben wiped his face with his shirt. "Whew, I'm hot! Let's get Pig and go swimming. Let's eat lunch, too—I'm starved.

"Oh, come on, Frankie," he added. "Even if we can't actually prove it, Pig's definitely not involved. He doesn't even *know* any gray dogs here."

"Right," Frankie said, heading for the house.

So why, she wondered as she went upstairs to get Pig, *am I still so sure he has something to do with what happened last night?*

And why do I get this strong, weird sense that there's a lot more to all this than just a dog going after some silly old hens?

CHAPTER 6

There must be a way. Pig stared at the words on his computer screen. *There must be. It's unpredictable this way, too risky—*

He jumped, startled. Frankie had come in, wrenching the door open without knocking. Quickly, before she could see what was on the screen, he shut down the computer.

"Hey, Pig," she said, "I'm going to the pond with Ben. We're going to have a picnic. Come on—grab your bathing suit!"

Swim! The coppery taste of panic rose in Pig's throat. *No, can't swim! Mustn't. Danger—danger!*

"Um—no—no thanks," he sputtered, ducking as Frankie took his bathing suit out of his drawer and threw it at him.

"What is *wrong* with you?" she demanded, hands on hips. But she looked worried, too.

41

"If I didn't know better, I'd say you were chicken. But you like swimming, you know you do."

"Not anymore," he said. "It's boring."

"Ha! Chicken, that's what you are. Scared of salamanders, I bet—and leeches—and snakes!" She paused, almost as if she was hoping he'd get mad.

But he wasn't angry. He *was* afraid, though he didn't understand why. Not of leeches or snakes—no, he was full of terror at the thought of going into the pond, even though he remembered that he'd liked swimming once. He'd liked the coolness of the water against his skin, the speed....

"I dare you." Frankie picked his swim trunks up off the floor and dangled them in front of him. "Chicken! I dare you!"

Pig gulped, swallowing his fear—or trying to, anyway. "Oh, okay," he snapped, grabbing the suit from her and shoving her toward the door. "I'll meet you there."

The swimming pond was small and shady, bordered on three sides by birches and a cluster of graceful weeping willows near where the brook fed it. On the fourth side, a small sandy beach sloped gradually down to the clear water. Lily pads floated lazily on the pond's surface near the opposite shore, with round buttercup-yellow water lilies nodding beside them. Frogs croaked from a thicket of reeds at one side. A large boulder, spotted with gray-green lichen, rose in the middle of the pond. It was steep-sided, but flat on top—a good place to dive from or just sit on and think, Pig remembered.

Pig had liked diving once; he remembered that clearly. But now, standing at the edge of the pond with Frankie, Ben, and Thrip, with the picnic basket in the shade behind them, he still felt an unreasonable sense of foreboding. He felt odd near Thrip, too—the dog kept shying away whenever he was nearby. *The way Mouser's been doing,* he thought.

Of course they shy away. That's part of it. Maybe—maybe water-fear is, too.

Small price to pay, though, for the speed...

"Last one in is a steamed pickerel!" Ben suddenly shouted.

"Steamed pickerel!" Frankie exclaimed. "What happened to 'rotten egg'?"

"Please," said Ben. "This is a chicken farm, remember? No rotten eggs here. Unless it's Pig," he added, looking at him. "What's the matter with you? Do you *want* to be a steamed pickerel?" Ben sprinted down to the water.

"I don't feel like swimming," Pig said. "I'll wait for you guys." He turned away as Ben plunged in and swam for the rock, with Thrip close behind him.

"Does your arm hurt?" Frankie asked, holding back. "That's it, isn't it?"

"No. Well—yeah, sure. It hurts a lot," he lied.

"Water's good for aches, Mom says."

"That's hot water," Pig answered. "Go ahead, Frankie." Deliberately, he walked over to the picnic basket and sat down on the ground beside it. "I'll guard the lunch."

Frankie shrugged and waded into the pond, then swam out to Ben, who was treading water. Thrip, panting, paddled in circles around them both. Pig watched while Ben threw a stick for the dog and then beckoned to Frankie. While they were playing with Thrip, Pig checked out the lunch basket contents: peaches, cookies, bologna sandwiches, unfortunately with lettuce…

Meat, he thought, pulling a slice of bologna out of a sandwich and cramming it into his mouth.

That's better. More meat. He reached for the next sandwich.

As he reached for the next sandwich, he saw Frankie and Ben swimming for shore. But after eating another slice or two of bologna, he lay back, the wolf-pelt cap over his eyes.

But suddenly—

"Now!" he heard Ben shout, and he felt the cap fall away as he was jerked roughly to his feet. Ben was yanking on one arm and Frankie on the other.

"Wh-what? Huh? But—" Pig sputtered as they pulled him down toward the pond. When he felt his feet touch the water, he screamed. "No, no, no, no!" he bellowed, thrashing free of them. While Ben and Frankie stared at him openmouthed, Pig took off back toward the farmhouse, running faster than he'd ever run in his life, the taste of panic again in his throat.

CHAPTER 7

Burning—burning—feet are burning—can't bear it—oh—ouch—ouch!

But as Pig's feet dried, the burning stopped, and by the time he'd reached his room and switched on the computer, they felt fine again. Normal, even.

Yes—here it is!

Pig stared at the words on the screen:

CHARACTERISTICS
Hairiness
Paleness
Eyebrows straight across
Wounds remaining when in human
    shape
Image not in mirror
Fear of bodies of water, especially
    around time of full moon
Animals uneasy around

Pig clicked on "Fear of bodies of water, especially around time of full moon," and leaned forward intently, reading the words as they appeared on the screen:

> Werewolves, like witches and other
> supernatural creatures, often shun
> bodies of water, for they won't sup-
> port them. Lake, pond, sea, and river
> water burns some werewolves, and if
> a werewolf enters any of them, it will
> sink like a stone and drown.

Whew!

Pig leaned back in his chair, feeling more than a little weak.

I was right not to go in. Wow, was I right!

He'd have to trust his instincts from now on.

"What's wrong with him?" Ben asked, staring after Pig. Thrip stood next to Ben, panting.

"I don't know." Frankie walked determinedly away from the shore and picked up the lunch basket. "But I think I'd better go find him."

"Wait." Ben followed her.

"Huh?"

"Well, if it was me," he said, "I'd be kind of

embarrassed if I'd freaked out like that. Maybe we should leave him alone. Maybe"—Ben looked longingly at the lunch basket—"we should eat first and then go after him. I'm sure he'll be okay, Frankie. Maybe something bit him when his feet hit the water. A crayfish or something."

"Are there crayfish in this pond?" Frankie asked dubiously.

Ben shrugged. "I don't know. There might be." He bent over the basket, rummaging in it. "Here. Have a sandwich—oh, gross! Look at this, Frankie. He's eaten the bologna out of at least two sandwiches."

"Gross is right." Frankie looked disgustedly at the limp, squashed bread. Since when did Pig eat only *part* of a sandwich?

"There are a couple of good ones," Ben said, handing her a sandwich that was still complete and taking another for himself. "I don't know about Pig," he said, settling back and taking a bite. "I don't think he has anything to do with the chicken problem, but I don't remember him ever being this weird."

"Neither do I," said Frankie. She quickly finished eating and stood up, wiping her hands on her shorts. "I'll take the basket back," she said. "Pig's had time to calm down by now, and I want to find out what's going on with him." She hesitated. "Maybe it'd be better if I went alone."

"Maybe it would," Ben agreed. "Thrip and I'll take a hike around the pond." He stood up. "Come on, Thrip!" he called. "Tell Dad I'll be along in a little while, okay, Frankie?"

"Okay," said Frankie. "See you later."

Frankie walked rapidly through the woods, the picnic basket in one hand. It banged awkwardly against her legs, but she hardly noticed it. She hadn't wanted to make a big deal of it to Ben, but she was more worried than ever about Pig. Sure, he'd been annoying before, and she'd been mad at him, but he'd never acted like *this*. And she still wasn't convinced he wasn't involved with the "chicken problem," as Ben called it.

Maybe there *was* really something wrong with him. Maybe he was going crazy, or maybe he *had* been sleepwalking the night before, as Aunt Trina had suggested. That would be bad enough, although if he had been scaring the chickens while sleepwalking it wouldn't really have been his fault.

But what about the gray dog? And why had Pig screamed when they'd tried to put him in the water? No, Frankie thought, going up onto the porch. Something was very strange.

Pig's scream had been one of pure terror.

The door to Ben and Pig's room was closed. That was a promising sign, Frankie thought as she knocked; at least Pig was probably in there.

There was no answer, so she called, "Pig? Piggy, you okay?"

Silence.

"Hey, let me in," she called. "It's Frankie."

Still no answer. She slowly opened the door.

Pig was scrunched down in front of the computer, his eyes practically glued to the gray screen.

"There you are, Piggy," she said, trying to sound casual. "What are you doing?"

Pig jumped when she touched his shoulder, as if he'd been concentrating so hard he hadn't heard her come in. He hit a couple of keys, switched off the computer, and turned around. "Oh, I—I—er..." he stammered. "I...had something I had to finish, so I thought I'd better do it. I thought of it all of a sudden. That's why I left."

"Oh, right!" Frankie sat on the edge of Ben's bed. "All of a sudden, when we were about to throw you in the water?"

"Well, how would you like being attacked like that? Anyway, I do have to get this done," he said, turning back to the computer. "My Special Project. Do you mind?"

"Yes," said Frankie carefully, not believing him, "I do. What *is* your Special Project, anyway?"

"Nothing much," he said vaguely.

"It can't be nothing much," she argued, "since you're spending so much time on it! It looked like you were planning a garden or something, before. I saw this list of stuff—plants, mostly, it looked like."

Pig glanced uneasily at the dark screen. "Oh, that," he said, sounding nervous.

"Yeah, *that*. Come on, Pig, what's going on?"

"Frankie," Pig said angrily, turning toward her, "I don't cross-examine *you* about everything you do, do I? So why are you cross-examining me?"

"Well, excuse *me!*" Frankie stood up, exasperated. He certainly didn't seem scared anymore. Maybe he'd just acted that way so he'd have an excuse to get back to his precious Special Project. "I was just trying to look out for you." Then she noticed a shadow on his face; she took a step or two toward him, to see it better. "You'd better go wash," she told him. "You've got smudges on your forehead.... No," she went on, looking more closely at the skin above his nose. "No, those aren't smudges—whoa, Pig, that's hair!" She reached out and touched Pig's forehead. "Holy smoke! It's like—like your eyebrows are...spreading!"

Pig ran his hand over his eyebrows, smoothing down the hair. "Better?" he asked.

"No," Frankie said, swallowing against the uneasy feeling that suddenly gripped her stomach. "No, it isn't. Piggy, this is weird! I mean, it's not normal. Maybe you're sick or something." She sat down on Ben's bed again, dazed. "Maybe we should ask Aunt Trina to get hold of Mom and Dad. Dad said we could radio them on the boat in an emergency."

Pig stared back at her, and for a moment Frankie thought he was going to agree. But then he set his jaw firmly and said, "No. Look, could you just go away?"

"No," she said. "No, I couldn't. Not until you—"

Pig leaped up out of his chair. "I said, go away!" he shouted. "Just go away, Frankie. Nothing's going on, and even if something was, it'd be none of your business. How many times do I have to say that? Now get out of here!"

CHAPTER 8

Frankie walked slowly outside, to where Ben and Thrip were admiring a complicated stick-and-bramble barrier Uncle Joe had woven in front of the chicken yard fence.

"In Kenya," Uncle Joe was explaining, "people of the Masai tribe build thornbush fences to keep lions out of their villages and away from their cattle. I thought I might take a page from their book. We don't have the same kind of thornbushes, of course, but these old raspberry and blackberry canes"—he pointed to them—"are pretty lethal. I figure if thornbush can keep lions out, then blackberry canes ought to do the trick for dogs and coyotes. What do you think?"

"Looks great, Dad," said Ben.

Frankie watched Thrip, who was sniffing along the edge of the thorny barrier as if trying to see whether there was a way through.

"I've reinforced the whole thing," said Uncle Joe, "not just where that hole was. And I think—"

A horn blared then, cutting him off. Frankie turned to see a heavyset man in a straw hat climbing out of a battered brown pickup truck that had just pulled in to the driveway.

"Afternoon, Joe," the man said, strolling over to them. Frankie noticed with interest that he had a fancy-looking camera slung over his shoulder, with little leather film canisters fastened to its strap.

"Afternoon, Clarence," said Uncle Joe. "This is my niece, Frankie Davis, come to stay for a while. Frankie, this is one of our neighbors, Mr. Hutch. Mr. Hutch takes pictures for the local newspaper when he isn't tending his sheep. Frankie's a photographer, too, Clarence."

"Good for you," Clarence Hutch said, touching his straw hat politely. "Great hobby, isn't it?" He turned to Uncle Joe. "What in thunder are you doing to your fence, Joe?"

"Coyote-proofing it, I hope," said Uncle Joe. "They do this in Africa against lions. Well, something like this, anyway. I figured the same technique ought to work against coyotes or dogs or foxes or whatever busted into my chicken yard last night."

"You, too?" said Mr. Hutch. "That's what I came to see you about. I caught one slinking around my south pasture last night bothering the sheep. It was a coyote, all right—no mistaking it. A large one. I went out because my dog was whining something awful. He wouldn't go with me, though—first time that's happened. But I got a good look at the critter. Long, gray, and mean-looking. I got a good look at its eyes, too. Odd eyes. Kind of intelligent."

Frankie thought of Lobo's eyes. She guessed one could call them intelligent.

Then, uncomfortably, she thought of Pig's eyes as he sat in front of the computer and as he'd stared at her just about each time she'd questioned him....

"That does it," Uncle Joe was saying. "Sounds like a coyote to me. I'm glad to have it identified, anyway."

"Now, we've got to stop it," said Mr. Hutch, "before it does some real damage. I can't afford to lose any sheep, and you can't afford to lose any chickens." He strode over to Uncle Joe's thorny barrier and poked it with his finger. "Ouch! Good idea, this fence—almost as good as barbed wire, I guess. But I can't very well put thorns around all my pasture land."

"No," said Uncle Joe, "I guess you can't."

"But," Mr. Hutch continued, "I can get my rifle out and shoot that animal dead. And you better believe I will."

CHAPTER 9

"There's a bag of cement mix in the barn," Ben whispered to Frankie that night after the dinner dishes were done and everyone else had left the kitchen. "It's a powder. All you have to do is mix it with water. We could mix some up and stick Lobo's paw in it, like you said. Then we can compare the mark it makes to the paw prints we followed."

Frankie hesitated, even though she was anxious to prove that Lobo was the culprit. The idea of sneaking up on that big dog wasn't something she relished. Besides, another idea was slowly forming in her mind—and because of it, she wasn't at all sure Pig should be left alone at night.

"Frankie, Ben!" Aunt Trina called from the living room. "Come join us. Joe's got a new song he wants you to hear."

57

"Coming!" Ben called. Under his breath he said to Frankie, "Let's meet in the barn at midnight, okay? I'll be working on my star chart for a while tonight anyway." He opened the freezer. "I'll bring a bone," he said, taking out a package wrapped in paper and plastic and putting it in his pocket. "This was for Thrip's birthday, but we can get him another."

"Okay," Frankie said, "but I—I've got a new idea."

"What?"

"Children!" Aunt Trina called. "Joe's waiting!"

"Later," Frankie whispered, hanging up her dish towel and following Ben to where Aunt Trina and Uncle Joe were sitting in front of the fireplace. Pig, looking pale and preoccupied, was just coming in from the porch.

Aunt Trina got up when he came in and put her hand on his arm. "Paul, dear," she said, "I'd like you to drink a mug of warm milk before you go to bed, to help you sleep more soundly. Okay?"

"Okay," Pig said with a shrug.

As Uncle Joe tuned his guitar and started singing, Frankie watched Pig carefully. He was gazing at the window. The nearly full moon shone through it, casting silver light onto the windowsill, where Aunt Trina had put a small pewter pitcher of yellow flowers. The flowers glowed in the moonlight, and Pig, Frankie noticed, couldn't seem to take his eyes off them. Or was it the moon he was looking at?

She wasn't sure.

Carefully, Pig turned away from the computer and looked toward Ben. Was he asleep? He'd gone to bed while Pig was still working at the computer. Pig remembered that because he'd been careful to block Ben's view of the monitor with his body even after Ben had closed his eyes.

Ben's chest moved evenly up and down as he breathed, and his eyes were tightly closed. His breaths were coming slowly and deeply—

He's asleep. It's safe.

Pig quietly got up; already he could feel his skin start itching, as if the hairs were just under the surface, anxiously waiting to grow.

He stooped and put on his high-tops, leaving them untied so he'd be able to kick them off quickly. This time he remembered to take off his watch; he put it in his top drawer so Ben wouldn't see it lying on the bureau if he got up. But he didn't notice that he'd left the computer on.

Stealthily, Pig scooped up a handful of green

ointment from the bowl on his night table and transferred it to an empty cat-food can. Then, taking the can and the wolfskin cap, he crept out of the room—but darted back to stick his pillow and a rolled-up blanket under the covers. He'd almost forgotten!

Slow down, he told himself. *Don't do anything stupid.*

He left the room again and went carefully down the stairs. He'd memorized which ones squeaked—including the ones leading down from the porch—and he remembered to avoid them. He skirted the chicken yard, giving it a wide berth; it wouldn't do to startle the hens before he was ready.

Stupid chickens—noisy—wake people up.

He could feel his brain slowing down as he entered the woods, his human thoughts thickening as his animal impulses grew stronger, even though he hadn't yet completely changed.

The clearing was bathed in moonlight, and Pig shivered a little as he stripped. The ointment was cool on his skin, and it soothed the itch. And the soft wolfskin cap warmed his head.

"Far, far away," he said softly, rubbing the ointment carefully over his arms, his legs, his face, *"under the bright moon..."*

At the end of the spell he felt the shrinking, the curling, the sudden pain as the hair grew and his limbs and body and head changed shape. He dropped to all fours. A moment later the change was complete, and at last, his eyes gleaming red and his sharp teeth glistening in the moonlight, he stretched luxuriously, and ran.

Freedom—speed—yes!

But—

Hungry—so hungry!

He'd have to go back to Mr. Hutch's place. *More meat,* Pig thought as he loped comfortably along, not hurrying now, sliding smoothly through the underbrush at the side of the road. There weren't many cars, but when one approached, he froze and waited, motionless, till it passed. He got so he could smell them coming as well as hear them. The wind was right—and besides, his sense of smell was getting stronger than his sight.

Almost there now—

But suddenly he stopped, sniffing, his muzzle high, his nose twitching. A wonderful fragrance came to him on the wind: fresh, rich, tantalizing...

Nose still twitching, mouth dripping saliva, he trotted forward, then wheeled away from Hutch's, deep into the woods along a well-used path. He smelled people now, and something acrid—smoke?—but it didn't matter; the good smell was stronger—

In the darkness ahead he saw a flickering light and heard laughter.

People! Boys—boys and a man—sitting—a—what's it called?—a tent, a—a campfire—

"Almost ready, sir," one of the khaki-clad boys said to a tall, bearded man, also in khaki.

"Good, Jones, good. I'm starved."

There was a chorus of "Me, too!" and talk about a long hike, about getting lost and finally finding camp again.

But Pig-wolf barely heard them. He was staring at a stump a little distance away from the campfire. A small boy was beside the stump, and on it was a sheet of foil, crinkled and sparkling in the firelight. On the foil—

Meat. Raw, red meat.

"Just about ready for the hamburger now, Mark," a boy near the fire called. "Bring me that flat thing, too. You know, the spatula?"

The small boy sitting beside the stump nodded and looked around on the ground nearby, where there was a pile of paper plates.

Pig-wolf stepped closer. The hair rose on his neck, and his breathing slowed. His legs stiffened and his eyes were riveted on the small boy.

Just three more steps. One...

"The spatula's not here," the boy called, straightening up. "Hang on a minute. It must be in the tent."

Two...

"Well, go get it, for Pete's sake. Hurry up!"

"I'm getting it, I'm getting it!" the boy shouted, turning toward the tent.

Three!

Pig-wolf lunged forward, snatched the raw hamburger, and ran.

The small boy's scream echoed through the silent woods.

CHAPTER 10

At a quarter to twelve that night, while Frankie was still figuring out how to get Ben to listen to her theory before trying to get Lobo's paw print, she heard Ben's voice outside her bedroom door.

"Psst! Frankie! Wake up! Let me in!"

Frankie rolled sleepily out of bed and opened her door. "Huh?" she asked, rubbing her eyes.

"It's time," Ben said, hurrying inside. "And Pig's not in his bed. It's rumpled, like he slept in it some, and the pillow and blanket are in it again."

Frankie wasn't surprised, but her stomach churned with fear all the same. She knew she should have tried to keep an eye on him!

Ben continued. "The computer's on, and

there's something really weird on it. I guess Pig forgot to turn it off. Come and see."

Her stomach still churning, Frankie followed Ben to his room.

Pig's bed was as Ben had said. His clothes were in a heap on a chair.

"The cap's gone, too," said Ben, also looking at the chair.

"What?"

"You know. That wolf-pelt cap of Dad's. I swear I saw it hanging on the bedpost earlier. Now it's not here."

"Did Pig go to bed when you did?" asked Frankie. "Before you got up again to go out at midnight?"

"No. He stayed up for a while after I went to bed, in his pajamas, fiddling with the computer again. I thought he was asleep when I got up to meet you. But I saw the computer was on, so I went over to his bed to tell him, and that's when I saw he was gone."

Frankie nodded absently, her eyes already on the screen. Whitish letters stared out at her:

Far, far away, under the bright moon,
In the wide space under the stars,
Birch and oak and stream watch

As the circle forms and the ancient
    words are spoken,
And as we apply the essence, the
    sacred essence,
Giver of freedom, of life, of power
    and strength.
Then at last we run, we run, we glide
    under tree,
Around bush, over grass and stone,
Coming at last, at long last, under the
    moon's fullness,
To the place we desire, to the taste
    we desire,
To the reward.
Moon, O moon, give me life; watch as
    I seize my true freedom!

Ben looked over her shoulder. "Weird, isn't it?"

"It sure is."

Ben laughed. "Maybe he's trying to be a writer, and the effort is making him into a sleepwalker instead."

Frankie found she couldn't laugh. "This is better than anything he could write, though. English has never been his best subject."

She went over to Pig's bed again. The bowl of yucky-looking greenish ointment was still on his night table, but the scooped-out place in the middle seemed a little bigger.

Frankie held up the bowl. "Do you know what this is?"

Ben wrinkled his nose. "Nope," he said. "But it sure stinks."

"Looks like there's less of it than yesterday," Frankie observed.

"Maybe he's got some disease he's not telling us about, and that's his medicine. Maybe that's anti-sleepwalking stuff!" Ben suggested.

"Maybe," Frankie said. "But if that was true, Mom would've told me, and there'd be a prescription label on it, and it'd be in a plastic bottle or a tube instead of in a bowl, and—"

Thrip's loud bark from downstairs cut her off. The bark was immediately followed by frantic squawking from the henhouse.

"Come on!" Ben shouted, bolting into the hall.

"Be right there!" Frankie dashed into her room, grabbed her camera and its flash attachment, and tore down the stairs into the yard. If her theory was right, she'd need proof. Even if she wasn't right, it would be helpful to have a picture of whatever—or whoever—was raiding the henhouse.

Ben and Uncle Joe and Aunt Trina were already outside, standing near the driveway.

Uncle Joe was holding Thrip's collar, and Thrip was shaking. "Let's all watch," Uncle Joe said softly. "I think the animal's probably trying to get through the fence. I know Clarence said he was sure it was a coyote, but I want to see for myself before I do anything rash, like shoot it. You know, in case it *is* someone's dog. Very quietly now—very quietly…"

On tiptoe, all four of them crept forward. No one, Frankie noticed, had to restrain Thrip—he was walking as far behind Uncle Joe as he could, whimpering softly.

"Would someone please take this dog back to the house?" Uncle Joe said in an annoyed whisper. "He's obviously not going to be any help."

"I'll go," said Aunt Trina. "Funny," she added, "Thrip's never been a coward before. Come on, Thrippy, there's a good boy."

Thrip didn't seem to need any urging.

Suddenly Frankie caught a movement near the fence, and she poked Uncle Joe before lifting the camera to her eye. "Over there," she whispered. "Look."

Uncle Joe nodded and put out his hand, preventing Ben and Frankie from going any closer.

Sure enough, through the viewfinder Frankie saw a low body, larger than she'd expected, creeping with its belly close to the ground. The animal was slinking along the perimeter of Uncle Joe's thorn fence, sniffing, as if hunting for a break in it. The dog or coyote was gray, all right, just as they'd thought. And it *did* look an awful lot like Lobo, Frankie decided.

Maybe, Frankie thought excitedly, snapping a picture, *it* is *Lobo after all.*

"I'll be darned," Uncle Joe breathed, so softly Frankie barely even heard him. "That's the biggest coyote I've ever seen! More like a wolf! And he didn't seem to notice your flash, Frankie. I think I've outsmarted him with the fence."

"He does look like Lobo, though," Frankie said, still following the animal in the viewfinder as he walked along the fence, sniffing and every once in a while trying to dig under it or through it.

"We saw Lobo today," Ben explained. "Frankie and I. To—um—check, sort of. And he really does look like this animal."

"Maybe, but I'm sure this is a wild animal," Uncle Joe said stubbornly. "A wild animal, raiding farms—which does mean he'll have to be shot."

"Yeah," said Ben, "but wouldn't Mr. Taylor make a lot of trouble about it if it did turn out to be Lobo and you shot him instead of—I don't know—turning him over to the dog officer or whoever takes care of that kind of thing? You know, officially?"

Uncle Joe sighed. "You're probably right," he said. "It's just that it'd be a lot quicker the other way. Look, there he goes now—toward the Taylors', I have to admit. But I still think he's a wild animal."

Frankie adjusted her shot as the animal loped off toward the woods. Before he left, though, he turned and looked at them, his eyes gleaming eerily red. "Straight into the camera," Frankie said—a little shakily, for the animal's eyes looked disturbingly familiar.

"I got a great shot, Uncle Joe," she said as they went back to the house. "Wait'll you see. I bet you'll be able to tell if it's Lobo or not."

"Good work, Frankie." Uncle Joe patted her shoulder. "Clarence Hutch has a darkroom. We can probably go over to his place in the morning and develop your film." He held the kitchen door open.

Aunt Trina greeted them at the door with mugs of cocoa, and Thrip wagged his tail sheepishly at them from his mat near the stove. "I'm sure glad it's you and not your sleepyhead brother who's the photography nut," Uncle Joe said to Frankie, sipping his cocoa. "I guess he slept through this, too, huh?" Suddenly Uncle Joe looked worried. "He *was* in bed when you came out, Ben, wasn't he?"

"Oh…uh, yeah," Ben said, after glancing at Frankie. "Yeah, he was."

Frankie didn't dispute him. It seemed to her that Uncle Joe had enough to worry about. But later, when they went upstairs, both she and Ben saw that the pillow and blanket were still piled in Pig's bed.

"I guess we'd better not try to get Lobo's paw print tonight," Ben whispered. "But I'll wait up for Pig."

"Me, too," said Frankie, her mouth dry with fear. What she was thinking didn't seem possible.

But it fits everything that's happened, she thought nervously. *I've got to find out more— about what I'm thinking about.*

Even if it's impossible.

What if it's true, though?

CHAPTER 11

Frankie woke with a start when she heard Pig's voice. She shot out of bed and found her brother in the hall with Ben, yawning and rubbing his eyes. "I don't know," he was saying to Ben. "I told you that already."

"Well, you'd better take a shower," Ben said, "before Mom sees you!" He gave Frankie a significant glance and whispered, "Sorry I couldn't stay awake. But he's in his pajamas and it looks like he's been sleepwalking, the way Mom said."

"I couldn't stay awake either," Frankie said, staring at her brother. He had huge smudges on his face, and his hands were black. There was even dirt under his nails. It was obvious that he'd been outside, and she agreed with Ben that it certainly looked as if he'd been sleepwalking. But why would a sleepwalker have dirt under his nails, unless—

Unless he'd been digging.

Under a fence, maybe.

"You go on to breakfast," Frankie said to Ben, putting a hand on Pig's arm. "I'll be right down."

"Pig," she asked carefully when Ben had left, "do you really not know how you got dirty?"

"Blast it, Frankie," Pig said angrily. "How many times do I have to say the same thing?" He stomped off to his room.

Blast her, Pig thought, pulling off his pajama top and throwing it on the floor, hardly noticing the dry leaves and thorns caught in the fabric. *Blast Frankie, blast Ben, blast everyone! Who cares if I'm dirty? Stupid thorn fence—scratched my nose...*

Pig felt his nose with his hand and then glanced in the mirror.

He stared—not at his reflection, but at the mirror's reflection of the room.

There was his bed, and Ben's, and a corner of the computer.

But even when he put his scratched and dirty face right against the glass, and then his grimy hand and arm, he couldn't see himself in the mirror at all!

CHAPTER 12

At breakfast Uncle Joe and Aunt Trina were cheerful, despite the disturbing events of the night before. Pig, Frankie noticed, was unusually quiet—and unusually hungry, even for him, reaching across the table for bacon before anyone could pass him the plate or help themselves.

"The hens weren't as upset this time," Aunt Trina said, serving pancakes. "I even found a few eggs this morning. That thorn fence really did the trick."

"It sure did," said Uncle Joe. "Hey, Paul, leave the rest of us some bacon, will you?" He poured syrup on his pancakes. "Those Masai really know their stuff. Still," he went on, "we've got to do something about that animal, coyote or Lobo or wolf—though that doesn't seem possible. Whatever it is, anyway. Not everyone can build a thorn fence."

"How about an electric fence?" asked Ben.

"Clarence Hutch has part of one," said Uncle Joe. "But he ran out of money before he finished it. I'd like to take your film over to his house today, Frankie. Clarence said it's fine with him. I sure am anxious to see those photos."

"Me, too," said Frankie, helping herself to syrup, but watching Pig out of the corner of her eye. He didn't seem aware of anything but his food. He also seemed to have forgotten how to hold a fork, grabbing it awkwardly in his fist the way a baby would instead of holding it in his fingers.

An hour later, everyone except Pig, who'd disappeared into his room after breakfast, crowded into Mr. Hutch's darkroom, waiting for Frankie's roll of film to develop.

Frankie leaned over the developer tank as the images started to appear. She glanced quickly at the photos she'd taken earlier on that roll—the farmhouse, Aunt Trina in her garden, Uncle Joe with his guitar on the porch, all of them in the living room, the pile of bloody feathers that first night…She peered closely at the henhouse pictures.

There seemed to be some kind of weird mistake. The henhouse was pretty clear, showing in the moonlight as it had the night before, and so was the thorn fence along which the animal had run and sniffed.

But there was no animal!

"Well," said Uncle Joe, obviously trying not to sound as disappointed as Frankie was sure he was, "maybe you just didn't snap it quickly enough, Frankie."

Frankie shook her head. "He was there a long time," she said. "He didn't leave till after I took the second picture, the one of him looking right at the camera, remember?"

"That must be this one." Ben pointed at another henhouse photo. Again the henhouse showed, but there was nothing else in the picture—as if the animal hadn't been there at all.

Or as if he was invisible, Frankie thought, mystified. *But that's impossible—we saw him!*

"Could it be his color?" Uncle Joe asked.

"He *is* gray," Aunt Trina put in, "and the background's sort of gray, too. Maybe he just doesn't show against it. Could the flash have bleached him out?"

"I doubt it," said Mr. Hutch. He gave Frankie

a funny look. "Are you sure you know how to work that camera?"

"Of course she does," Uncle Joe said loyally. "You saw all the other stuff well enough, didn't you?"

"Well," said Mr. Hutch, patting Frankie's shoulder, "we've all seen the coyote clearly enough in the flesh, that's for sure. I'll get him next time I see him, too. You can count on that."

"Or I will," said Uncle Joe grimly. "I've got my gun all ready."

There it is again, Frankie thought. *That feeling about Pig. And if my impossible idea is right...* "What—what if it's a dog?" she blurted out; it was the only thing she could think of saying to discourage the men from trying to shoot. How could she possibly suggest to them that the marauder they were hunting wasn't a real animal at all, especially when she wasn't sure she believed that herself? "I mean, if it's a dog—well, as Ben said, its owner would get mad, and—"

"I checked with the dog officer early this morning," Uncle Joe said. "He said it's okay to shoot even if it is a dog, since it's threatening farm animals."

"Oh, it's not a dog," said Mr. Hutch with great certainty. "There's no way it's a dog." He grinned, and clapped Uncle Joe on the back. "We'll have ourselves a real old-fashioned coyote hunt, eh, Joe?"

"Right," said Uncle Joe. "I guess we'd better."

CHAPTER 13

"For Pete's sake, Pig," Ben grumbled that night, yawning, from his bed. "Get some sleep! What time is it, anyway?"

"I don't know," Pig said dully. He'd already put his watch in the drawer, put the cat food can in the cap, and put the cap under the covers on his bed. The night was overcast, and he was sitting by the window, staring out and waiting.

"Well," Ben said crossly, turning over, "I'm going to sleep."

But Pig had the distinct feeling that Ben wasn't planning to sleep at all, that he was deliberately staying awake—

Spying.

That's it. He's spying. He and Frankie.

I'll fix them, he thought as the moon floated out from behind a cloud. He felt the hairs on the back of his neck bristle. *I can! Fix them!*

The itching of his skin became more insistent.

Fix—hungry—hungry—

There'd been only macaroni and cheese with salad for dinner, no meat. Pig's mouth felt hollow, and his stomach growled with desire for meat.

Farm near Hutch's. Sheep. Cows—too big. Geese—feathers—blagh!

Sheep. More sheep than at Hutch's. Safer, too, maybe.

Pig glanced at Ben. He seemed to be sleeping now. To make sure, he went over to the bed and looked down at his cousin. The moon burst from behind a cloud, flooding the room with light. Pig's scalp prickled; his fingers curled. Lips pulled back, he leaned over and sniffed at Ben.

Ben stirred slightly in his sleep.

Pig bent lower—then pulled away.

No. Not now. Not yet. Let him sleep.

Awkwardly, his hands oddly cupped and pawlike, Pig seized the cap, stuffed the pillow and blanket under his covers, and left.

Pig-wolf loped along the road, once more freezing when cars came along. But there weren't many; it was very late. The moon slipped in and out of clouds, but it didn't matter now that he'd changed—and besides, he could smell his way.

A squirrel raced across his path and he lunged for it. Missed.

Too small, anyway.

Too small.

He passed Hutch's, where the thing had stung him. Then another car came; Pig-wolf froze while it passed, then moved on. Gradually, the woods thinned.

Almost there now.

He paused, panting a little from excitement, when the woods changed to pasture.

Cows—too big—need sheep...

He went on, sniffing the air. There was a fence, another pasture—and there they were, lots of them.

It was an open fence, just a few strands of wire, not like the chicken yard one. Effortlessly, he slipped between the wires.

Easy, so easy!

Sheep—meat. Hungry—so hungry!

One ewe moved away from her companions, nibbling at the grass.

Pig's wolf lips curled upward in a sinister grin. *Yes—yes—stupid sheep, away from the others. Good!*

Slowly, silently, he stalked her, slinking along the edge of the field, careful to keep downwind of her.

One ewe, a different one, raised her head nervously and bleated. Then they all bleated, noses twitching, and bunched together nervously.

So Pig-wolf ran and leaped toward the lone ewe, cutting her off from the rest of the flock. He ran beside her as she ran, his head turned toward her. He could see the wild terror in her eyes, hear her labored breathing.

He opened his mouth, ready to lunge for her throat.

And then suddenly a black-and-white whirlwind appeared from nowhere and hurled itself at him, growling, baring its teeth—

No! Sheepdog!

The dog barked.

Then there was a loud crack and a searing pain.

Pig-wolf fell to the ground.

CHAPTER 14

"Where is he?"

"In bed, Frankie, I swear," Ben said the next morning when they met on the stairs on the way to breakfast. "I don't think he went out."

"Then why's he asleep?" Frankie asked. "Why isn't he up? You know how he is about food!" She ran to Ben's room, and yanked open the door.

Pig stood there, fully dressed, his hands in his pockets and a forced-looking smile on his face. Frankie noticed dark circles under his eyes.

"Good morning," he said, sounding very stiff and formal. "Sleep well?"

"Y-Yes," Frankie stammered, staring at him. Was it her imagination, or had his eyebrows grown even closer together? "Did you?"

"Like a rock," he said—but his voice sounded strained and tense. "Let's go eat."

"Okay," she said. "Sure. Let's."

But as she followed him down the stairs, she noticed that he seemed to be having trouble walking. She didn't dare ask why, or what had happened. Part of her was afraid he would snap at her...and part of her didn't want to know.

All that day, Pig favored his leg, trying to hide it and his pain from the others. At first when he'd been shot he hadn't known what hit him, only that he had to get away. He'd scrambled to his feet, snarling at the sheepdog that was nipping at him, and then he'd limped off to the woods on three legs. The dog started after him, but then someone whistled from near the farmhouse, and the dog stayed behind with the sheep.

Safe in the woods, Pig-wolf had flopped down and curled his body around to smell his wound. It was long, running from haunch to heel on one hind leg, and salty with blood.

But he didn't smell or feel bone as he licked it as clean as he could.

The wound became stiff as it dried, and the leg hurt when he moved, so he lay there till he sensed the moon was about to set; then, slowly, painfully, he made his way back to Dunmead Farm.

He got to the clearing just as the sun rose, and he crashed through the woods to the farm in his own shape. Thrip growled, as usual, and shrank away when Pig went through the kitchen, but that didn't matter. Ben was still asleep, though he stirred when Pig came in and crawled into bed, stifling his moans of pain. Later, when Ben got up and left the room, Pig quickly threw on his clothes and dabbed the dirt off his face with an old shirt.

He'd managed to wash his hands downstairs right before breakfast—he knew Aunt Trina would have noticed the dirt on them—and he'd managed, just barely, to get through the day, sitting under the beech tree and reading, mostly. The air was hot and sultry; no one did much except the necessary chores.

Dinner was cold tuna salad on rolls— because of the heat, Aunt Trina said. Pig gulped a sandwich, but it didn't do much to quell his hunger pangs, which were really growing. He asked Aunt Trina when they were going to have meat again.

"Probably tomorrow," she said cheerfully—

and then there was a clap of thunder and everyone cheered as the storm broke, chasing the heat away.

Now Pig lay in bed dozing, trying to sleep—but his leg was throbbing badly and it was harder than ever not to moan. Images kept flitting across his mind—and smells, wonderful earth smells, forest smells, animal smells. They teased his nostrils: *squirrel....rabbit...chicken...fat, succulent sheep...*

Leg hurts—feels hot—hungry still—need meat, fresh red meat. Last night—almost—get one for sure next time. Getting better at it, much better.

Pig's limbs stirred; despite his aching leg, he longed to run.

When will it stop raining so I can see the moon, so the moon can see me?

Leg hot—so hot!

Rain pounded on the roof all that night and was still streaming down the next morning. Everyone seemed grumpy, especially Aunt Trina.

"I don't know what to do with your brother, Frankie," she said when Frankie went down to the kitchen late for breakfast. Ben and Uncle Joe had already eaten and were out doing chores. "Honestly, I'm beginning to be very worried about him. I don't think he went out last night, but he won't get out of bed. He looks pale and he hardly spoke to me when I tried to wake him. Are you sure he doesn't have some kind of sleep disorder?"

"He never used to." Frankie took a deep breath. "I'll go see if I can get him up."

"When you do," Aunt Trina called after her, "I think I'm going to talk to him about paying a little visit to the doctor. We've got to find out what's wrong with him. And maybe I should get in touch with your parents, too."

Frankie went upstairs and found Pig huddled deep under the covers. But he was wide awake, his lips set in a thin line as if he were in pain. "Go away," he said through his teeth as soon as Frankie walked into the room.

"No. Aunt Trina wants you to get up. Now."

"Too bad."

"Come on, Pig." Frankie strode over to the bed and stripped off the covers. Pig grabbed one pajama leg, tugging it as if trying to hide his skin—only he was too late.

Frankie gasped.

A long red wound stretched from thigh to foot, puffy and angry-looking. Thick yellowish liquid oozed from one part of it.

For a moment Frankie just stared, and Pig

lay there waiting, with his eyes closed.

"What happened?" Frankie was finally able to ask.

"I don't know."

"What do you mean, you don't know? You can't get a—a big scratch like that and not know!"

"Well, I don't," Pig said angrily.

Frankie took his hand. "Piggy," she said softly, "you've got to let Aunt Trina look at it. There's pus coming out of it—it looks infected, Pig!"

"No."

"Yes! What about gangrene, amputations, being crippled for life?" Frankie curled one leg under her, twisted her face into a grimace, and hopped around his bed.

Pig laughed briefly, and Frankie smiled as he got up and limped to the door.

But Pig's good mood didn't last long. "Don't touch me," he suddenly snarled, lunging at Frankie when she tried to help him down the hallway.

She stepped back, her eyes wide with surprise and fear. "What's wrong with you?" she asked in a choked voice. "I'm getting Aunt Trina!"

Aunt Trina and Uncle Joe took Pig to the doctor right away. Frankie, Ben, and Thrip were left on their own, staring gloomily out at the rain.

"At least that animal didn't prowl last night," Ben said, restlessly pacing around the living room.

"No," said Frankie. "At least, I guess he didn't." *Pig,* she thought, *didn't go out last night either. As far as we know, anyway. But then how did he get that horrible scratch?*

"Mom got lots of eggs this morning," Ben said listlessly, turning away from the window. "Rain's so boring! I don't even want to work on my star chart. Do you know any good games?"

"Just dumb ones. Old Maid, Battleship, Authors, stuff like that. And checkers."

"I wish we had a computer," Ben said. Then he brightened. "Hey—we do now. Pig's! He must have some games, right?"

"Yeah," Frankie said reluctantly. The last thing she wanted to do was play a game—any game. She wasn't sure she really even wanted to find out what was wrong with Pig, because she knew that no one would believe her if her theory was right, and she had no idea how she could prove it or stop Pig in time to save him.

And maybe save some farm animals. She

shuddered. Or even people, too.

"Let's go see what he's got," Ben said, and raced up to his room. Frankie followed slowly behind.

"Maybe he's got some games on the hard disk; he told me he loads most things in." Ben switched the computer on, clicked to the MENU, and scrolled. Frankie peered over his shoulder.

Suddenly she leaned forward and grabbed Ben's arm. "Stop!" she said. "Wait a sec. Scroll back."

"Huh?"

"I thought I saw something weird." A knot had formed in her stomach, and part of her didn't want to see what she was seeing. *But I can't stop now*, she thought, *not with Uncle Joe and Mr. Hutch planning to go out with guns....I'll just have to find a way to prove it if I'm right.*

And then there it was.

"Stop," Frankie said. "Shove over." She sat next to Ben, grabbed the mouse from him, and clicked on a file labeled "Shapeshifting."

First to appear was the list of plants she'd seen on the screen before. Next came the odd-looking poem. Then there was a chart showing the phases of the moon for the summer months, with the day of the full moon and a couple of days before and after it circled. "Gibbous," Ben muttered, "as well as full." And finally came a list of odd statements:

CHARACTERISTICS
Hairiness
Paleness
Eyebrows straight across
Wounds remaining when in human shape
Image not in mirror
Fear of bodies of water, especially around
    time of full moon
Animals uneasy around

REQUIREMENTS
Animal skin (especially wolf, etc.)
Full moon and days around
Ointment
Spell

BACK
Knife on nose
Reverse spell
Sunrise

While Frankie was staring at "Animals uneasy around" and thinking of Mouser and Thrip, Ben laughed and said, "Leave it to Pig to study something weird. I bet he believes in ghosts, too! Let's go back to the menu. I think I saw something called 'Forest Castle.' That sounds like a game."

"Pig," said Frankie slowly, "is too serious to study something that isn't real."

"Oh, come on, Frankie. You don't believe…"

"I don't know what I believe," said Frankie—although she was almost certain of it now, horrible though it was. "But I'm not going to say this doesn't mean anything." She turned around to face Ben. "Look," she said, "I saw that list of plants the morning after the first night Pig stayed out. And I saw the poem the next time." She frowned. "And—and it says 'Ointment' here. Remember the gross stuff that's beside Pig's night table, in the bowl?"

Ben nodded. "Yuck," he said. "I sure do. Green. Like it's made out of grass or something."

Frankie snapped her fingers. "Right!" She went over to the bowl and sniffed it. "Yes. I thought I remembered that it smelled sort of like plants—plants! Like the list. Maybe the ointment was made out of the plants on the list! Maybe—Ben, maybe Pig made it."

Ben stared at her. "Oh, come on," he said. "Why would he do that?"

"I don't know. Well, yes, I think I do. Like— well, what's this file called?"

"'Shapeshifting,'" said Ben. "But I don't see what…"

"Shapeshifting," Frankie repeated. "Don't you get it? That must mean changing shape. Becoming something else." She put her hand on her cousin's arm. "Ben," she said, "I saw this old movie once, on TV. It was called something like *The Shapeshifters of Shiloh.*"

Ben laughed nervously. "Yeah? So?"

"So it was about this guy," Frankie told him, "who turned into a wolf every time the moon was full. He was a werewolf, Ben!"

Ben stared at her again for a moment, and then laughed. "Come *on*, Frankie! There aren't any such things."

"But suppose there are? Ben," she said, her voice very low and serious, "think about what's been happening. And think about the way Pig's been acting. Your father said the animal looked big for a coyote—was the biggest coyote he'd ever seen, anyway, more like a wolf, he said. And look at the list of characteristics: fear of bodies of water, hairiness, eyebrows growing across—his are; I noticed it the other day, and they've grown since then. 'Image not in mirror'—that's another. There are mirrors in cameras, Ben—and the pictures I took of the animal didn't come out, remember? Then there's the 'Requirements' list, too—maybe that's of things you need for changing your shape. The ointment, it said, and an animal skin. What about that awful green goo Pig's got? And your dad's wolfskin cap?

"Ben," she said, relieved at finally being sure enough to say it out loud, but horrified at the same time, "I think my brother's a werewolf!"

CHAPTER 15

A clatter from the kitchen told Frankie and Ben that Joe, Trina, and Pig must have come back. They pulled themselves together and went downstairs.

"There you are!" said Aunt Trina. "How about some lunch?"

"Um...sure." Frankie looked nervously at her brother, who was sitting at the kitchen table, his leg propped up in front of him. "How are you, Pig?" She tried to tell herself he was still Pig, no matter what else he'd become. Somewhere, underneath that, he was still Pig.

"He's going to live," said Uncle Joe, glancing up over the top of the local weekly newspaper. "But he's got to be careful of that leg for a while. The doctor said the wound looked like

95

a bullet graze, but he thinks it's a deep scratch from a branch. Trouble is, Paul doesn't remember it happening, do you, Paul?"

Pig shook his head, avoiding Frankie's eyes.

Frankie glanced significantly at Ben, who nodded slightly. *A bullet graze*, she thought, with a sick, panicky feeling. Pig had already been shot at!

"The doctor gave Paul some pills," Aunt Trina said, "to help him sleep more soundly."

"None of us'll be able to sleep soundly if we don't get that coyote soon," Uncle Joe remarked grimly, throwing the paper down on the table. "Look at this!"

Frankie looked over Ben's shoulder:

WILD ANIMAL SPOTTED
AT DOAN FARM

"It looked like a wolf, I swear it did," said farmer George Doan early yesterday morning when he burst, pale and shaken, into the Animal Control Office.

But, according to Stephen Merrill, Animal Control Officer, chances are it's just a big coyote.

"My dog went after it," Doan said,

"and I got a shot at it. I think I hit it, but it got away."

Tuesday night, according to George Fipps, scoutmaster of Boy Scout Troop 411, a wolflike dog snatched some hamburger from the troop's campsite.

The animal was seen at Dunmead Farm that night, too, near the chicken yard, which owner Joe Brooke has protected with a thorn barrier, "like those the Masai tribe use in Africa," Brooke explained. "That's why I built the fence," he said, saying that the night before, the animal had attacked his chickens, wounding one of them. It chased Clarence Hutch's sheep the same night.

"The important thing is not to panic," Merrill warned, "but to take sensible precautions. Coyotes rarely attack people and almost always hunt at night. Everyone should be careful to keep kids and pets indoors after dark. See to your fences, and stay alert. Report anything strange to me. So far, the animal hasn't killed, and we have every hope of getting it before it does."

Frankie felt a chill spread over her entire body. The *whole town* was after Pig now.

"We've got to do something," she said to Ben later, out near the barn where they could talk without being overheard. Aunt Trina had sent Pig to his room to rest. "We've got to stop him before he really gets hurt."

"Or before he hurts someone else," Ben said. "I mean, aren't werewolves dangerous to people once they—well, get going?"

"Yeah," Frankie said, remembering the movie she'd seen. She thought of Pig's harsh-looking eyes, and shuddered.

"We've just got to watch him more carefully," Ben said, "and keep him from going out at night."

"Maybe," Frankie agreed. "But we haven't done too well at that so far. Besides, aren't werewolves supposed to be super strong? The one in that movie I saw was."

"There's a lot of old rope in the barn. If we wait till he's asleep, maybe we can tie him to his bed."

"I guess we could try," Frankie said. She couldn't think of a better idea. "He'll be mad, but if he doesn't escape, at least he'll be safe."

"Yeah," Ben said grimly. "*He'll* be safe—but will we?"

Got to get out—got to get out—got to get out...

Pig thrashed restlessly in his bed all afternoon, drifting in and out of sleep. Aunt Trina brought him a tray at dinnertime: chicken soup and biscuits, no meat, no rich raw red meat, even though he could smell the pork chops she was going to broil for the others. But she said he was sick, that he needed soup instead. He gulped it down, but he was still hungry afterward and he only pretended to take his bedtime pills, holding them under his tongue till Aunt Trina left the room and then spitting them out.

Moon, moon, rise; let me see you rise....

He put the wolf cap on his head and the cat-food can with the ointment in his pocket. He could hear Uncle Joe singing downstairs. *Stupid songs...*

Then the moon came up. *Beautiful moon—*

Pig smiled at it; it had become his friend, his leader, his god, almost—but he had to wait. He knew he had to wait, even though he felt the change beginning; his body was ready for it even before he used the ointment. He felt the wildness growing inside again, the slowing of his brain, the sharpening of his instincts, the hunger, the longing for speed.... The hunger was hard to bear, harder each time. His mouth dripped saliva; his teeth ached, beginning to lengthen....

The door opened and the boy came in— what was his name? *Doesn't matter,* Pig thought, watching him with his eyes mostly closed so the boy would think he was asleep....

The boy came in slowly, carrying something in his hands—what? A rope, a long, heavy rope!

No, Pig thought, every muscle alert now, *no rope, no—no tying up. He wants to do that— to tie me up—won't let him—mean plump boy.*

Plump boy!

Hungry—so hungry!

Glancing cautiously at Pig's sleeping form, Ben laid the rope, neatly coiled, beside his bed, then tiptoed to his door, where Frankie was waiting.

"I think he's asleep," he whispered. "Maybe we'd better do it now."

Frankie shook her head. "No—it's too risky," she whispered back. "Your parents are still awake, and Pig's bound to wake up and struggle. Let's just give it another hour, okay? Try to stay awake. Read or something."

Ben nodded. "See you in an hour, then," he said.

"Right. G'night—for now." Frankie padded down the hall to her room.

CHAPTER 16

"He's gone," Ben said, urgently shaking Frankie's arm. "I'm sorry. I must've fallen asleep. And he was wearing that wolf-pelt hat, and I think he took some of the green stuff. Frankie, I..." He looked embarrassed. "I'm sorry. We'd better go after him—hurry up!"

But Frankie was already out of bed, pulling her jeans on over her shorty pajama bottoms. She stuffed her feet into her sneakers and, grabbing a sweatshirt from the pile of clothes on the chair in the corner, raced after Ben. He called softly to Thrip, who was pacing restlessly in the kitchen, and they all burst out the front door just in time to see a pale figure disappearing among the trees at the edge of the farmyard.

It was Pig. Without saying a word to each other, Frankie and Ben followed him deep into the woods. Thrip, Frankie noticed, stayed well behind them, keeping them between himself and Pig.

"We're going to that clearing again, I bet," Ben whispered. And soon they were at its edge. Ben, who was in front, put his arm out, keeping Frankie from going farther. "He's stopped," Ben whispered. "We'd better not get any closer."

Frankie looked over Ben's shoulder and saw that Pig was partly behind a bush, wearing the wolf-pelt hat and carrying a long stick. While she and Ben watched, he drew a circle around his feet with the stick, then held his hands up to the full moon.

"Far, far away," he intoned, "under the bright moon..."

"It's the poem on the computer screen," Frankie whispered excitedly.

"Yeah," said Ben. "Wow!"

"Was I right?" Frankie turned to him, triumph briefly overshadowing her growing nervousness. "Or was I right?"

"I don't know yet," Ben said. "Maybe. So far, anyway. But—oh, gross! Disgusting! Look what he's doing now!"

Frankie looked and then grimaced. Pig was holding an old cat-food can, and was scooping out little green globs of something and rubbing them on his bare chest, his arms, his face, his legs.

"The ointment," breathed Frankie.

"Moon, O moon," said Pig, reaching the end of the poem, "give me life; watch as I seize my true freedom!"

With those words, his face started to change. Within moments, his ears became pointed and furry and moved to the top of his head. The shadows on his cheeks and chin and forehead turned into hair; his nose grew long, pointed, and black-tipped; and his arms grew hairy and his hands became paws. He seemed to crouch as his body became larger and leaner, covering itself with gray fur, and his legs lost their human fleshiness. He dropped—fell, really—to all fours, and his thighs turned into doglike haunches. His lower legs lengthened and then grew leaner till they were thin as sticks—but strong: Frankie could see the outline of sinewy muscle as well as of bone.

There was a furrow in the hair on one hind leg, as if a bullet had grazed it.

Last to go were Pig's human hands and feet, which slowly melted into large, sturdy paws with dark, curving nails.

The creature that had been Frankie's brother just a minute ago turned his head toward them. His tongue hung out a little as he panted, revealing long teeth. He raised his long nose and sniffed the air. His eyes, fiery red, shone eagerly in the moonlight—and Frankie moved back, groping for Ben's hand, which felt as cold and clammy as her own.

Then, limping slightly on one front leg and more markedly on one hind leg, Pig trotted all the way out from behind the bush, threw back his wolf head in the moonlight, howled, and ran out of the clearing.

"Wow!" Ben whispered shakily. Frankie still couldn't move or speak. "That's—that's Pig! I don't believe it!"

But it was true.

Frankie shuddered. Pig had turned into a wolf—a living, breathing, frightening, bloodthirsty *wolf*. And he was on the loose.

CHAPTER 17

Yes, now, yes, yes—food, meat, run—oh, wonderful moon—air smells good—fresh—sheep near—

Pig stopped, his wolf nose quivering, his tongue lolling.

People.

People and sheep.

Hunters?

Dog! Dog—

He dropped his head and stalked, stiff-legged, toward the dog smell—

And the dog, large and gray like him, sniffing the ground as he ran, burst out of the woods near the clearing.

With a single leap, Pig attacked, and the dog rose to meet him, snarling furiously.

Back at the clearing, Frankie couldn't move.

That—that creature, that wild, cruel-looking beast, it couldn't be Pig, not the brother she'd fought with and played with for as long as she could remember. That beast looked as if it could kill easily…happily, even. For a brief moment she wished Uncle Joe would come with his gun and shoot it.

But it is *Pig,* she told herself firmly, gathering her courage. *Locked in that werewolf's body is my brother—and we've got to save him!*

Frankie turned to Ben, who stood there looking stunned. Thrip trembled and whined softly behind him. "Come on," she whispered, touching Ben's arm. "Come on. We've got to stop him," she said more loudly, "before Uncle Joe and Mr. Hutch see him. Ben!" She shook him; he blinked at last, as if coming out of a trance. "Ben, come on!" She grabbed his arm and pulled him toward the edge of the clearing.

"Sorry." Ben finally broke into a run beside her. "Come on, Thrip! It's just that—well, you know. I—I still can't believe what we just saw. There's got to be an explanation. There's got to be—only there isn't—but oh, please, there should be," he gasped. "Frankie, I—"

"Shut up!" Frankie whispered fiercely, to stop his nervous babbling. She was pretty sure, from the way the underbrush was parted, that they were on Pig's trail, but she didn't dare slow down. She knew that she'd feel a lot better if she could only glimpse him— There! That looked like his tail, just ahead. "You saw the same thing I did."

"Yeah, but *how?*" Ben panted beside her. "It's impossible. We saw it, but it's impossible. Do we know where we're going? Oh—oh, no! Frankie! Frankie, look!"

Frankie turned to the side, where Ben was pointing. For a moment, her heart nearly stopped. There, next to the path, a limp gray shape—a wolfish shape—lay on its side, very still.

"Dead," Ben said, poking it gingerly with his foot.

Frankie's breath caught in her throat—and then she stepped back, stifling a scream, as the animal moved.

"Lobo," Ben whispered, stepping back with her as the big dog slunk away, limping, a bloody wound on its haunch.

Frankie felt an absurd desire to laugh, then sobered instantly. Relief that the animal hadn't been Pig, lying there dead, was quickly replaced by fear: Had *Pig* done that? Had her brother actually tried to kill Lobo?

"Come on," Ben said, touching her arm. "We'd better go on. We're pretty close to Mr. Hutch's place. His south pasture. I think—"

Suddenly two shots rang out.

Frankie suppressed another scream and grabbed Ben's hand. They took off, bursting into the unfenced pasture just in time to see Pig loping across it while a cluster of terrified sheep bleated frantically at the other end.

Frankie heard a male voice shout, "Missed him!" and then she saw Mr. Hutch run out from around the corner of the barn, carrying a rifle. He lifted it up, sighting along the barrel, aiming at Pig...Then he lowered it and rubbed his eyes, exclaiming, "That's no coyote, by ginger! That's a real live wolf!" He lifted the rifle again, sighted again, aimed—

"Pig!" Frankie screamed. "Run!"

Another shot covered her scream just as Pig darted into the woods again. Frankie couldn't tell if he'd been hit.

She ran faster, breaking out into the field as Mr. Hutch turned away. Ben and Thrip followed close behind her.

"He's going toward Dunmead," panted Ben, "or he was, anyway."

"Pig!" shouted Frankie again when they reached the woods—but she was so winded by then, her voice was weak. "Pig, stop," she moaned. "They've got guns! Pig, they'll shoot at you again!"

"It's no good," gasped Ben. "He's a wolf now—he can't understand! Watch out!"

Pig had turned and was waiting just ahead, facing them, snarling, teeth bared.

CHAPTER 18

*People—people stopping me—first the dog—
now them—that boy again—that girl, too—
seen her before—trying to stop me—have to
get them—have to have meat—meat—
meat—*

Frankie froze. Ben and Thrip, just behind her,
stopped as soon as she did.

Her first thought was relief that Pig didn't
look hurt. "Pig," said Frankie softly, her heart
pounding painfully in her throat, "Pig, it's me,
Frankie, your sister. And Ben's with me. Don't
you know us?"

The beast in front of them snarled in
response, his lips twitching over long, yellowish teeth. Stiff-legged, he stalked toward them.

Ben grabbed Frankie's arm. "He's going to
attack," he said in an oddly calm voice. "We're

going to be attacked by your own brother. Oh, my God, Frankie!"

"Easy, Pig," said Frankie, trying to keep her voice steady, and not taking her eyes off the angry werewolf's snarling face. His eyes looked right into hers, somehow not as angry as the rest of him seemed—maybe even a little frightened; she couldn't be sure. "Easy, Pig," she said again, holding out her hand, thinking she ought to approach him the way she'd approach a strange dog. But the werewolf lunged toward her. Frankie snatched her hand away and stepped back, nearly knocking Ben over.

Suddenly everything seemed to be happening in slow motion. She and Ben clung to each other in terror, and the werewolf gathered himself for a mighty leap, his sneering, vicious mouth open, ready to bite—

And then something hurtled past them, toward the werewolf, and threw itself on him, knocking him back mid-leap, throwing him down.

"Thrip!" shouted Ben. "Watch out! No, Thrip!" He let go of Frankie and they both ran forward.

But Thrip was doing fine. In fact, he had the werewolf pinned to the ground and was standing over him. Frankie and Ben both fell on the beast at the same time, grabbing legs, fur, anything to make the werewolf stay where he was.

"Pig," Frankie sobbed, holding the beast's front legs and chest. "Pig, listen to me. You're a werewolf, not a real wolf. Uncle Joe and Mr. Hutch are hunting you. Other people, too, I guess, by now. They've got *guns*; they want to shoot you! Like—like they shot your leg. You've got to change back into your own shape, Piggy; you've got to. Please! Before it's too late."

But Pig-wolf only snarled louder, bared his teeth, and gave a mighty heave, throwing Frankie, Ben, and Thrip aside as if they were weightless toys.

CHAPTER 19

Frankie froze, terrified, and closed her eyes. The words "He's my brother, my own brother!" echoed in her mind. She didn't know if she'd said them out loud or not. She also didn't know if the sobs she heard came from herself or from Ben. She just knew she wanted the whole nightmarish scene to be over.

Angry growls mingled with the sobs and grew louder, deafening; then moved away, then came closer, then moved away again.

It sounded like two dogs fighting, Frankie thought dully, only she knew it wasn't two dogs. *It's a dog and a werewolf, and the werewolf is my brother and he'll probably kill Thrip and then kill us, and all because we tried to keep him from getting killed himself....*

114

"Frankie."

That was Ben's voice, close to her. She felt something touch her arm. A scream caught in her throat, but then she realized that what had touched her was Ben's hand, not the werewolf's teeth, and she opened her eyes.

The first thing she saw was that the moon was setting and the sky was growing lighter.

Following Ben's pointing finger, she saw Thrip and the wolf that was Pig facing each other, obviously exhausted, no longer fighting but just panting, tongues lolling, sides heaving. Thrip was trembling. He was whimpering softly, and his torn ear was bleeding, but he stood his ground.

Pig seemed even more exhausted than Thrip.

Cautiously, Frankie walked toward him, again holding out her hand. Her mouth was dry with fear and her legs felt so weak she thought they might collapse.

Pig snarled at her, baring his teeth.

"Piggy, it's me," Frankie whispered, barely moving her lips. "Oh, please!"

Girl—afraid of me—girl—moon—where's moon?
Moon's going.
Girl—something familiar—who?

115

*   *   *

For a moment, a hundredth of a second maybe, Pig-wolf's glittering eyes softened, looking like Pig-boy's own.

"Pig—Piggy—I won't hurt you," Frankie whispered again.

He moved toward her. Frankie's pulse quickened. Was he about to attack?

"Watch out," Ben whispered urgently behind her. "Watch out—"

And then, with an earsplitting howl, Pig lunged toward her—but he swerved at the last instant, and fell, cowering, panting and shaking, under a tree.

"It's almost sunrise," Ben whispered. "Remember the 'Back' list on the computer? There were three things on it...."

Frankie racked her brain, trying to remember the list. Something about a knife, she thought, and—yes—sunrise, and one other thing—something about a spell...

"Look!" Ben whispered, just as Frankie became conscious of an odd whining. She thought it was Thrip at first, and then realized the sound was coming from Pig. And as the moon sank behind the outline of the forest and the eastern sky glowed with the dawn, he crept out from under the tree and slunk slowly back toward Mr. Hutch's farm.

"No, Pig," Frankie shouted, "don't go there!" But he wouldn't stop, so Frankie, Ben, and Thrip followed him.

People—dog—nice girl—won't hurt me—
No moon.
Sun! Sun's coming!
I—I'm changing—
The girl—no!
Frankie.
My sister.
I—I'm Pig. Paul Davis. I—
I almost killed my own sister. I won't—I can't—Never—
No—no—no!

Pig led them around Mr. Hutch's field and back to the clearing; as he walked, his muzzle shortened, and his ears grew rounder, and his front legs shrank into arms. As his gray fur melted into skin, he darted behind a bush in the clearing, and Frankie saw for the first time that his clothes lay there in a heap, with the wolf-pelt cap and the greasy cat-food can near-by.

A few minutes later, Pig stepped out from behind the bush, back in his natural shape again—but looking pale and shaken, as if he'd come back from the dead.

CHAPTER 20

"Thank you," Pig said a moment later, sounding more like himself than he had for a long time. "Thank you. I...It was awful—awful...."

He covered his face with his hands.

Frankie made him sit down on the ground, and she and Ben sat beside him. Thrip ran to him and, obviously no longer frightened, licked his face.

"I—I found this book," Pig explained, his voice shaking, "last spring in the school library. About werewolves. It was really neat. I thought it was, anyway. I started looking for other books—I even brought one here—and I put a lot of the information on the computer. I got so into it, I decided I'd try it myself, even back when we were still at home in Cambridge. I don't know why....I guess I just wanted to do something different, something

118

nobody else could do. I didn't think it'd really *work*, though. I just tried it for fun, sort of pretending it'd work. There are lots of methods...."

"We know," said Frankie. "We saw your notes on the computer. We saw the ointment, too."

Pig made a face. "Horrible stuff. You have to rub it on yourself in order to change. I was a were*dog* one night back in Cambridge, before we came up here. I figured that would be pretty safe. But when we got here and I found Uncle Joe's cap, I decided to be a were*wolf.* You need the hair or the skin of the animal you want to change into." He fingered the cap gingerly. "I'll be glad to give this back to Uncle Joe. I wasn't sure it would really work at first, but then it did. You go into sort of a trance. It's weird. I was never sure, when I was myself again, whether I'd been in animal shape or not. It was almost like dreaming—"

"Some dream!" Ben remarked. "More like a nightmare."

"No, it was great at first—the running, the freedom. I felt stronger than I've ever felt before. And chasing the chickens was fun. I wasn't going to kill them, at least at first I wasn't; it was just fun to scare them. But later I began wanting to eat them—or any meat—

raw." He shuddered. "I was hungry all the time—ravenous—for meat. That was the bad part. It scared me."

"Why did you keep on changing shape, then," asked Ben, "if it scared you?"

"It's sort of like what they say about being on drugs, I guess. Once you've changed, you want to change again, and you want to a little more each time, until you can't stop even if you want to," Pig confessed. "It takes you over, kind of."

Frankie thought again of the "Back" list on the computer. "Was it really just the sunrise that made you change back? What about the other ways?"

"I didn't try them. I didn't think I could. You need another person to tap you on the nose with a knife for one of them, and for the other, the reverse spell—well, I didn't see how I'd be able to say the spell backwards if I was in wolf shape, even though that's what some of the legends say to do. If I'd had to do that, I bet I wouldn't ever have been able to shift back. I'd have had to stay a wolf forever. Anyway, I found a special moon spell. If you use it to shift, you change back automatically when the sun comes up. It's a little risky, because you're never sure where you'll be then, and you don't want anyone to see you changing. And of course you can only use it around the time of the full moon."

"The days you marked," said Frankie.

Pig nodded. "Right. If I wanted to keep on changing, I'd only be able to do it a couple more times this month."

"And," Ben pointed out, "then you'd probably have only a couple more days to live, with Dad and Mr. Hutch and everyone hunting for you with guns."

Frankie reached for Pig's hand. "You won't do it again, will you?" she asked, searching his face.

"No. You got to me in time." He squeezed Frankie's hand. "And good old Thrip helped, too." He gave the dog an affectionate hug, and Thrip licked his face again. "Look at him. He knows I've given it up. That must be why he's not scared of me anymore."

"What do you mean, we got to you in time?" asked Frankie.

"Well, like I said, the more you shapeshift, the more you want to—unless you decide to stop somewhere in the cycle, sometime during the period when you can shift. If I'd shifted tomorrow and the next night, then I might never have been able to stop. Every time the moon was full, I'd probably have wanted to change, if you hadn't gone after me.

And then pretty soon I'd just change automatically, whether I wanted to or not. I'd already begun to feel that happening a little." Pig shuddered. "I did get—something—tonight, didn't I?" he asked in a small voice. "Did I kill it?"

"No," Ben told him. "That was Lobo, the neighbors' dog. You got him in the leg, but he's pretty tough. We saw him limp away. He'll be all right."

Pig shuddered again. "You keep a little bit of your human brain—at least, I did—even though it doesn't work quite the same way. And when I finally realized I was attacking you two and Thrip, I knew I'd stop. I never wanted to hurt you guys, but it was like I couldn't help myself. Then I sure wanted the sun to rise in a hurry!"

"Me, too!" said Frankie. And then she, Ben, Thrip, and Pig made their way back to Dunmead Farm.

It was past dawn when they arrived, but Uncle Joe and Aunt Trina were still asleep. "Just to make sure," said Frankie when she and the boys had tiptoed with Thrip up the stairs past Aunt Trina and Uncle Joe's room, "we'd better get rid of some of the stuff."

Ben held out his hand for the wolf-pelt cap. Frankie took the bowl and the cat food can, both of which still contained a little ointment, and washed all the remaining goop down the bathroom drain. Pig went into the back of Ben's closet, dug out the book he'd been reading under the beech tree, and handed it to Frankie.

"Disk, please?" she said with a smile.

Pig handed it to her. "I erased it from the hard drive already," he said.

Ben clicked the menu on. There was no sign of "Shapeshifters."

"Well," said Ben, "I guess that's that."

Thrip wagged his tail.

"One more thing," said Frankie. She went into her room, picked up Mouser, and carried her in to Pig.

Mouser purred happily when Frankie put her in Pig's arms.

*If werewolves don't scare you,
how about vampires?*

My Sister, the Vampire

by Nancy Garden

Thanks to unexpected events, twelve-year-old Tim and his sisters, Sarah and Jenny, are left on their own at their family's summer cabin. It seems like a dream come true.

But the dream soon turns into a nightmare. Bats—hundreds of them!—have invaded the house. Meanwhile, the kid next door is wasting away, haunted by terrifying nightmares. When Sarah develops the same symptoms, Tim realizes the bites on their necks are not from mosquitoes. Vampires are loose in Starfish Harbor. And Sarah's about to become one of them...unless the kids can find and destroy them fast!

A BULLSEYE BOOK PUBLISHED BY RANDOM HOUSE, INC.

**If you're looking for more thrills and chills,
why not step into the**

SHADOW ZONE™

The Shadow Zone can be anywhere. Next door.
At school. Even in your own bedroom. It's the
place where the everyday world meets the eerie
domain of vampires, werewolves, and ghouls...

Read these books in the **SHADOW ZONE** *series:*

Here's another creepy series from Bullseye Books:

BULLSEYE CHILLERS™
Camp Zombie
Camp Zombie: The Second Summer
The Changeling
Dr. Jekyll and Mr. Hyde
Edgar Allan Poe's Tales of Terror
Fangs of Evil
Frankenstein
The Mummy Awakes
The Phantom of the Opera
Return of the Werewolf
Shadow of the Fox
The Vampire